THE GLASS MOUNTAIN

THE GLASS MOUNTAIN

A NOVEL

LEONARD WOLF

THE OVERLOOK PRESS

WOODSTOCK • NEW YORK

First published in 1993 by
The Overlook Press
Lewis Hollow Road
Woodstock, New York 12498

Library of Congress Cataloging-in-Publication Data

Wolf, Leonard.
    The glass mountain : a novel / by Leonard Wolf
  1. Imaginary places—Fiction.   I. Title.

PS3573,0488G57
813'.54—dc20

ISBN : 0-87951-498-1

                                                                    93-15768
                                                                        CIP

Book Design by Bernard Schleifer
Typeset by AeroType, Inc.

This book is for Deborah
who always believed in it.

I

THIS is the place. The map of the flat world is all but made and I, fat Klaus, have made it, tracing with my boots its latitudes and longitudes in my ten-year search for Amalasuntha. With the exception of the ten-mile square to the north where she is, I have touched every inch of the world.

We are a thousand feet up in a room of a broken tower at the center of a plain that reels away in all directions until it collides with distant cliffs so high they would hurl an unwary man to his death. Far to the south there is a single snow-clad mountain whose jagged peak pierces the night sky.

The harelip, Fritz, lies on the torn bed and sleeps. His breathing, because of his torn lip, is difficult and loud and makes his snores seem painful.

The morning's earliest sunlight coming through the window opening in the tower room moves tentatively down the wall behind the bed. The debris of the harelip's struggle with the mattress litters the stone floor. Cockatoo feathers drift from one corner of the room to another. The moist odor of the dead billy goat in another corner mingles with the genteel pungencies of my mother's handkerchiefs. The corpse of the ape looks resigned and patient as, with its tiny hands balled into fists, it leans at an angle against a wall.

I got here yesterday. My white horse was at the end of its strength when I saw before me the tower looming on the plain. When I reached it at nightfall, I found Fritz already there. "I watched you so long as there was daylight," he said. "Then I thought I'd better come down."

I leaned on his shoulder as he helped me to dismount. He was harder to the touch than a rock.

I tied my horse to a dead catalpa tree that stood to the left of the tower and followed him through the small postern gate at its base. Inside, before I could get accustomed to the weak moonlight that reached the bottom of the shaft, I stumbled on him where he stood waiting for me before a spiral staircase.

"What's the matter?" I said.

He was courteous, but firm, "I thought you should know. There is only one bed at the top of the tower."

"Thank you. I don't mind." Despite the gloom, he found my hand and led me up the stairs. The climb, I soon discovered, was not easy. Heavy as I am, every button of my clothing, every ounce of leather in my shoes slowed me. Behind me, at a distance, there sounded the whickering of my horse. Before me, the harelip's shoes grated on the stone.

I pressed against the wall and followed the sound of his footsteps. I did not need to be told that there was a drop at my right. When we reached the top of the stairway I stepped into a room and saw the bed of which he had spoken. It was no more than a rusted iron army cot, narrow and broken. From six steps away I could tell that its lumpy mattress was stuffed with tundra grass. It was a dismal bed, but I was so tired I yearned to sit on it.

Almost as if he had heard my thought, he said, "Sit if you like," and made what was for a man with so clumsy a body a rather gracious bow. I had to hold my own fat bulk carefully as I made my way across the moonlit space to the bed, which, I could now see, was covered by a reed coverlet that gave off an odor of something dead or dying, mingled with the smell of soaked hair.

I would have drawn back, but in ten years of difficult wandering, I had encountered worse vicissitudes. I was not about to give up a chance to rest because of some torn reeds and a marshy smell.

I sat and was immediately glad. The heaviness in my legs and the ache in my shoulders drained away. At the same time, I felt vague shapes thrusting or rolling against my fat thighs. I put my hand over a gap in the reed coverlet and touched something soft and wet. I snatched my hand away.

"You're right. It's not a nice bed," the harelip said, "but it's what we've got." In the moonlight that framed him I saw what a tall broad-shouldered man he was. He had a craggy head with hair that looked crisp—as if curled by lightning. His hands were large and not very clean. His eyes, set deeply in their sockets, were black.

In the increasingly bright moonlight I could make out the marks near the heels of his boots where his spurs had been. I caught a glimpse, too, of his pale ankles. His doublet clung to his shoulders and flapped over his ribs. His hose were baggy and badly drawn on over his strong legs. I could see whole islands of flesh showing through rents in the cloth.

"You're very kind," I said.

"As you would have been had you gotten here first." His voice was hoarse. His torn upper lip impeded his speech and yet what he said was surprisingly clear.

I made a deprecating gesture and would have said something but just then we heard a whinny.

"My horse is hungry."

My old white horse was now a gaunt and damaged animal, but he had long been faithful. It is true that he had failed me at the glass mountain, but I could hardly blame him for that. Still, he had carried me to the very brink of the summit before his strength gave out. Now, swaybacked and lean, he was tied to the bare catalpa tree at the base of the tower.

"He'll find precious little to eat down there," the harelip said.

"What about your horse?" I said, gesturing toward his boots.

"Dead, as I entered the valley. I made the last eight hours across the plain on foot. She was a good mare."

"I'm sorry," I said. For a while we were both silent. The harelip stood as before, his back to the moonlight. I supposed we were both thinking about horses, but when he spoke he said, "Do you want to tell me how you got here?"

Of course I was tempted. I had a long night ahead of me. Would it not be a pleasant way for a couple of travelers to while away the hours? So I almost said, "Yes, what a good idea," but I became sensible of my danger in time. This tower was the final staging point of my journey. If he was here and I was here, was it not certain that we were rivals for Amalasuntha? And so I said, "I would prefer not to."

His shoulders drooped. Rubbing his nose with a dirty forefinger he studied his boots. Then, breathing hard, he said, "I only meant. . . . We are so far from everything here. . . . I thought that I . . . that we . . . "

His manner touched me with remorse. It struck me that if I had not been so tired, if I had just wakened from a restful sleep with the sun shining through a high window, or if we had met beside a mountain brook after a long journey, we might well have spent a couple of cheerful hours trading adventures.

On the other hand — and here I hardened by heart — I had my journey to protect. I had been searching for Amalasuntha for a full ten years. Tomorrow, one of us would find her in the ten-mile square to the north. I meant that one to be me. I started to make a stern reply, but the harelip, as if he had heard something, turned away from me and leaned out of the window opening on which he stood and peered down. When he turned back, he said, "I'm sorry to tell you, but your horse is dead."

"What?"

"Come. Come and see," he said. Turning sideways, he made room in his moonlit alcove for me. I shuffled across the room and climbed into his alcove with him. The empty plain looked rinsed in moonlight. Far below, my white horse made a stark silhouette where it lay, its forelegs drawn up to its chest, its hind legs held in the stiff, lascivious position death requires of animals. Ravens, who had come from only God knows where in that desolation, were already dotting the body.

So that was the end of my horse, my companion from the day my brother and I left our castle to ride for Amalasuntha.

II

WE were two princes. First, there was Hans, my handsome younger brother. Twenty-two and blond. He was tall and imperious. I, Klaus, was two years older, with brown eyes and straight hair that hung in limp streaks across a moist forehead. Given to humility, I was also a walking prison of meat: fat, very fat. In my dreams, I was slim and lithe and climbed silver ladders to the sun.

We rode for Amalasuntha soon after my mother died on that night in the banquet hall when she met the Persian. He was a kindly old man who, accompanied by his saffron vendor, a scruffy ape and a dazzling white cockatoo, went from one market town to another telling fortunes. His bad luck was that he met my brother, whom he offended. Later, when my mother met the Persian, she was enchanted by the tall, handsome old man whose appreciation of her made her dying seem like the last pleasure of her life.

My brother Hans and I buried and mourned her for an uneasy week. Without her, the castle chimed like an empty wine glass. As the days went by, Hans grew more and more restless until one morning he mounted his black charger and rode off into our mountain forest. Though he said nothing, I knew what he was up to—vengeance for my mother's death. He meant to find the Persian and the saffron vendor.

He found the young woman. When he was done with her, he flung her aside and mounted his black charger. It was as he was riding home that he found, tacked to a catalpa tree, the notice about Amalasuntha that was to change our lives.

That notice, bordered in red and green and printed in huge block letters, said:

THE ROYAL PRINCESS
AMALASUNTHA
OFFERED IN MARRIAGE
TO THE PRINCE WHO SUCCEEDS
IN RIDING HIS HORSE
TO THE TOP OF THE
GLASS MOUNTAIN

Below, in smaller letters, were the details: Amalasuntha's father, the king of a nearby country, had had a glass mountain built at whose tip he had set Amalasuntha, his only daughter, the most beautiful woman in the world. Her father offered Amalasuntha's hand to any prince who could ride to the top and bring her down from the mountain. When Hans read that unsuccessful princes who survived their failure on the glass would be summarily executed, his mind was immediately made up. He galloped home and announced that he would ride for Amalasuntha.

What was I to do. I was older than he. Though I was fat, I was strong. I had a good horse. Under the circumstances, there was nothing for me to do but to offer to ride with him. For a wonder, he agreed.

Here, Fritz, the harelip, who was standing at my side looking down said, "I know how you must feel about your poor mount. I loved my horse, too."

"I wasn't thinking of my horse," I said and went brusquely back to the bed.

"I was thinking of mine. She was a modest brown nag, but as you know, I lost her."

The word "lost" burrowed like a mite into my brain where it twisted and untwisted memories of Hans and Amalasuntha riding down the glass; of the Persian with my mother in his embrace; of myself, fat Klaus, with my gartered legs floundering above the saffron vendor.

I made a move as if to rise but the harelip said, "Stay where you are." He spoke so sharply that I obeyed. He went on, "You've come a long way, but then, so have I. . ." Behind him, there rose the sound of ravens busy with my horse. Their beaks made a distinct *click, click, click, clack*. "Like you," he said, "I rode for Amalsuntha. I rode . . . " He pounded a fist into his palm. "Oh, it was hopeless. It was all wrong. I had no natural talent for success, but I rode."

Below the murmur of his voice, I heard the slow beating of my heart.

"I rode," he went on. "Once I . . . that is . . . there was a time. . . . Yes. Once upon a time . . . I rode . . . "

III

" . . . THERE was Amalasuntha," Fritz, the hare-lipped traveler said. "The most beautiful woman in the world." He interrupted himself. "You know, I used to kiss what was said to be her portrait, but always carefully so as not to wet the image with my lips. In the picture, her face was oval, pale and thoughtful under the coil of her black hair. She wore a green silk gown that flowed away from her like water from a pool. Her slim shoulders were held back, and she sat alert and straight."

Fritz paused. "Are you surprised at my candor? When one is loathesome . . . "

I shifted my great weight and said, "You're not loathe-some."

"That's civil of you, but you could hardly say anything else." His voice took on a hopeful lilt. "Are you sure you don't want to tell me your story?"

"I'm quite sure." To mollify him I said, "You seem to be trembling. If you're cold, you may have my cloak."

"Very well. Let me have it. It will be something to be warm." I stood and threw it to him. He flung it over his shoulders, then turned to look down at the plain. In my huge cloak, he looked shrunken, penitent. "Thank you," he said.

I had no objection to his being comfortable. As for Amalasuntha, he could know nothing about her beyond the common rumors. It was only to me she had revealed herself.

There was a cough and he asked, "May I go on with my story?" Setting his shoulders against the moon-drenched stone, he resumed: "Amalasuntha's capital swarmed with young men. No city in the world ever had an air of more desperate gaiety. We were young and full of spirit, dizzy with bravado. For us, the edge of doom was four miles out of town and it was made of glass.

"The mountain was breathtaking. It was so clear that sometimes we lost sight of it and were only able to sense its presence when high-flying ducks or swans wheeled and checked above the unseen impediment. The sight of death was never so beautiful.

"Every day men mounted and rode to glory. Each day's end saw them broken, huddled in the wheelbarrows the king's men used to haul the failed riders to the tundra west of the mountain where they were buried.

"No wonder that the bravest of us yielded to an instinct for delay. While we waited, we feasted or drank or gambled or took casual comfort (those who had no impediment like mine) in the brothels of the town – anything to delay that final ride.

"Most of the time we studied horses. Daily, after the animals had died on the glass we compared their performances, studying scrupulously the smallest equine detail. We knew to the milligram the weight of their horseshoes, the shades of difference in the colors of their saddle blankets, the amount of pull each rider exerted on his girth. We were entranced by hooves, fetlocks, manes, withers, noses, ears, chests and nostrils. We made charts and tables from which we deduced omens and signs. We became masters of the statistics of failure. So engrossed were we by the equestrian details that sometimes it almost seemed as if we had forgotten that there was an Amalasuntha on the mountain. What counted was the last height record established by some doomed horse before it finally slipped and fell.

"Each day scores of young men, disgusted by delay and ashamed of the pressure of fear in their stomachs, joined the Line of Approach that led to the mountain.

"My brother Baldur and I had been in the capital a week when we met the Persian. Baldur had toyed with the vices of the town and I had served him as a casual pimp.

"You will hardly believe this, but I could be useful to my brother. It's strange, but the revulsion women felt for me managed to rouse their lust. Not for me, of course. That was unthinkable. No, what I'm talking about was a sort of free-form lust, an unfocused erotic energy that found its target in my handsome brother. A woman who turned from the sight of my face and caught a glimpse of Baldur's Greek-god profile melted immediately into his arms where, mistaking his skill for passion, she achieved a hasty ecstasy.

"It was, then, as Baldur and I sat over a bottle of wine in the largest of the taverns that the Persian drew up a chair beside us. I was intrigued by the contrast between his age and the powerful muscles in the old man's arm and the vigor in his gray eyes as he watched my brother carelessly fondling the young woman who lay coiled in his lap. The old man stroked his white beard thoughtfully, then he said, 'Does she belong to you?'

" 'In a manner of speaking,' my brother replied.

" 'In what manner, please?' asked the Persian, pronouncing his words as if our language were difficult for him.

" 'She is mine while I want her and for so long as she amuses me.'

"Oh, it was unfair. Baldur, who was already indifferent to her, had her while I who yearned to breathe the fragrance of her auburn hair had to sit in the shadows lest she catch sight of my face.

" 'Sell her to me,' the Persian said. " 'Beautiful as she is, I think she does not stir your blood . . . ' And then, before either of us knew what he intended, he bent and kissed her forehead. At the touch of his lips, she opened her eyes and saw his lined old face. Baldur at first regarded the scene with revulsion, but when the sleepy woman reached out a hand and took the Persian's wrist, Baldur averted his eyes. The woman put her cheek against the palm of the old man's hand and held it there as if that was where it belonged. I could smell how her odor changed from saffron to musk to myrrh. When, finally, she sank back into my brother's lap, I could feel that she had caught a clear glimpse of the Persian through the opium mists that clouded her brain.

"The Persian studied my brother for a while; then he said, 'Come, Prince. Sell her to me. You have no use for her. You'll be riding for Amalasuntha soon. You have neither the desire nor the time for this sleepy head.'

" 'Why do you want her?' Baldur asked. 'You are old. Her youth will mock you.'

"The old man passed a finger over the blue circles under the sleeping woman's eyes and said, 'She looks unhappy in her sleep. I would like to wake her.'

"'Ha! That's all? Tell that to my brother Fritz. He's a simpleton and may believe you.'

"'I do,' I said fervently. 'I do.'

"'Thank you Fritz,' the Persian said, but, though I hoped he would keep talking to me, he turned back to Baldur. 'Since you put a question to me, let me ask you one. Why do you want Amalasuntha?'

"'Who says I want her?'

"'You are here in her capital. You mean to risk your bones.'

"'I ride against the mountain. It is an unclimbable mountain which I mean to climb.'

"'So? You think you can succeed where so many have already died?'

"Baldur drew himself up, 'Skill, old man. I am one of those who can read dark secrets.'

"The Persian looked narrowly at him. 'A fellow practitioner?'

"Baldur laughed so loudly the wine in our glasses trembled. 'Guess what you like.'

"My heart sank because I saw what was happening. The old necromancer had recognized the young one and now they were circling each other looking for points of advantage. While they strutted and preened, neither of them would remember that it was I who had found the lovely sleeper.

"At Baldur's bidding, it is true. I found her for him on one more weary errand to make his days pass pleasantly. She lay on an odorous shelf in the darkest of the town's brothels, her almond-shaped green eyes feverish with opium. Stretched out in the half-dark, she turned in a long spiral of sleep. The drug coursed in her blood and kept her warm and unconscious, but when I poked her, she roused herself sufficiently to reach her arm out.

"It was very dark. She was in her dream and could not see my mouth so she responded to my touch while all around us the cavern rustled with the bird cries of other lovers. She put her cheek against my shoulder and added her somnolent voice to the *chhhhhp chhhhhr* of tongues and sweetness. Moved by something in her dream, she caressed and soothed me, distantly content to be my love. She would have kissed me, but someone struck a match and even opium could not disguise my face.

"Did I say it was a twilit cave? The heavy odors of her body were gathering to her lips; she was nibbling my ear and whispering, 'This is better, eh . . . better than the woman on the mountain whom you will never see or touch. Better, eh?' My mouth was ready, my torn lips were as pursed as I could make them, but the match flared and she fell away from me."

The harelip paused and rubbed the bridge of his nose wearily. "You know, I own a mirror. I had no right to be surprised that she fell away from me. Perhaps, even, I had no right to feel a pang of regret. What I finally did was what I had been sent to do. I gathered her in my arms and carried her to my gifted younger brother whose lips were whole. He used her or abused her. Sometimes, when he had nothing better to do, he let her lie in his lap and stroked her indifferently. She, drifting on opium fumes, dreamed on.

"Now, he and the Persian were dickering for her. 'Well, old fellow. Suppose,' Baldur said, 'suppose I was willing to sell her, what will you pay?' As he talked he pinched and prodded her. She moved an arm, an eyelid, a toe.

" 'When you are ready to sell, I will make an offer.'

"Turning to me, Baldur said, 'What do you say, Fritz? Shall we throw this old dog a bone?'

I was sick of his handsome bearing, his graceful disdain. I was sick of his successes, his irony and his vast indifference. When I remembered my mother's monument: the labor of the pentangle, the torrent of birds, and that other glittering mountain rising to the sky I was sick of Baldur to the very bottom of my soul. Still, one does not easily shake the habit of obedience. Covering my mouth, I said, 'Yes, but he looks poor. Make him name his price first.'

"Turning his blue eyes full on me the Persian said, 'Wisely spoken, Fritz. Tell me, do you also ride against the mountain?'

" 'No," I whispered. 'I don't care about the mountain. I ride for Amalasuntha.' Looking at him, I felt as if he and I were alone. The hubbub in the tavern died. My unhappy infancy, my mother's imperfect love faded from my memory. Almost, almost, I could feel my wounded upper lip stiffening, healing.

" 'Aren't you ambitious?'

" 'Yes,' I said. 'For Amalasuntha.'

" 'You,' he chided. 'You, with your ruined face.'

" 'Because of my ruined face.'

" 'I see. Hmmm . . . ' He stroked his beard, then turning to Baldur he said, 'The price? Yes, the heart of the matter. I don't have much money, as you may guess. On the other hand, it just may be that I can help you to your heart's desire.'

" 'Heart's desire!' Baldur sneered. 'Do you have an amazing horse? Or the secret for riding on glass?'

" 'No. But perhaps I have something better. Listen. In exchange for your sleeping beauty, I will set each of you a riddle. Master it, and you may have your heart's desire.'

" 'No,' I cried. 'I'm not clever. I never can guess riddles. I would be sure to fail.'

" 'Yes," said Baldur. 'Tell us your riddles, shabby old man.'

" 'Careful,' the necromancer said. 'No need to be offensive. You are a young man much spoiled by the habit of success. But even you can fail.'

" 'Your riddles, old fool. Speak. Our bargain is made.'

"A cold look came into the Persian's eyes. 'Prince, take care. It is written, *Honor the white hairs of age*. You are in the very capital of unsuccess. No need to provoke the fates.'

"My pale brother looked paler. The beggarly old man had offended him. For a moment, I was sure there would be bloodshed; then, to my surprise, Baldur merely shrugged and said, " 'Never mind. The woman will be yours when we have heard your riddles.'

" 'A riddle then, for each of you, as I proposed,' said the Persian. The young woman in Baldur's lap shifted so that a lock of her hair fell across her face. The old mountebank reached over to brush it aside but Baldur growled, 'Hands off, old man, she is not yours yet.'

" 'No. Very well, then. Listen. Once upon a time . . . '

" 'I'm listening,' said Baldur, settling back in his chair.

" 'Now it begins,' I thought bitterly. 'Clever Baldur, my handsome, fortunate brother who has the habit of success and who can solve riddles, will get Amalasuntha, while I . . .'

" 'Once upon a time,' the Persian's voice sounded long-ago and faraway, 'a prince was riding east to west across a distant country. On a sunny day, at noon, he came upon a great city surrounded by a fruitful plain. The prince paused on a hill to gaze at the splendor of the city's golden towers, and at the extent and strength of its walls. In all his wanderings, he had not seen a city so lovely nor a country-side more abundant or serene.

" 'What was his surprise, then, to observe a mournful procession coming toward him from the city's gates. A hundred persons, men and women, moved to the sound of flutes and oboes, of drums and tambourines. When they neared the prince, the people knelt and did obeisance, but when they had done, he saw that their eyes were filled with tears.

" 'When he asked why they made him so ceremonious and so sad a welcome, the leader of the procession replied, "Sir, this lamentation, as well as this joy, is made because of you."

" ' "Why me?" inquired the prince.

" ' "Because not three days ago, our king, may his name be blessed—our king died and now, according to our custom, we must choose another. Since you have come within the prophesied time, it is you whom we must have for our king."

" 'When the prince had well considered what he had heard, he counted himself as one of the fortunate princes of the world. "I am honored," he told the leader of the procession. "And I agree to be your king. But why is there so much sorrow mingled with your joy?"

" ' "Ah sir, sir. Having accepted to be our king, there remains only that you pass the single test required of you. And this is why we groan, why we lament."

" ' "A test! What test! Have you not chosen me to be your king?"

" ' "Certainly we have chosen, but as yet, the fates have not, and our choice must be ratified by them. For that to happen, you must submit yourself to a simple test of endurance. The chance that you will survive the test is one in two. Not bad odds in this world but, because you are handsome and young, we could wish them better. If you do survive the test, you will reign over us in love and happiness. If you die, we will bury you. And that is why we weep even as we rejoice."

" ' "Is the test absolutely necessary?" asked the prince.

" ' "Alas, both custom and law forbid any changes in the method by which we choose our king." At this, the people in the procession waved mournful flags and sang a "Miserere" and "Hail to the King."

" 'The prince, too proud to be afraid and too greedy to give up so remarkable a kingdom, said, "Bring on your test and you will have your king."

" 'The leader of the procession said, "See, prince . . . On this cart is the skin of a horse. It is brown and tough and old. On that cart, you see a goatskin mottled black and white, and it too, is tough and old. Our law is clear. You must choose either the skin of the horse or that of the goat. Then you will be sewn into the skin you choose after which you will be left here on the plain to pass the night. Entirely enclosed by the skin of your choice, your task will be to get free before dawn. If you are not free by then, you die. Now, which of the two skins do you prefer?"

" 'Bitterly, the prince said, "How can I tell by looking?"

" ' "Therefore we weep for you," the leader said. With that, the music sounded; a thrill of lamentation went through the crowd. The prince, unwilling to indulge in the folly of a useless regret, bowed his head to destiny and chose a skin. When the people had sewn him into the skin of his choice, a guard was set on it.' The Persian stopped.

" 'That's it?' Baldur asked. 'That's the riddle I must solve?'

"The Persian busied himself around the woman in my brother's lap. 'Yes,' he said.

" 'And I am not to know which skin the prince chose?'

" 'No. As Fritz says, you are a clever man. You will no doubt guess what you need to know. Now, I will take this young bundle . . . '

" 'Keep your hands to yourself. You haven't told my brother his riddle.'

"The Persian sighed and shook his head. 'Why don't we spare him, prince. You and I, we are men of judgment and experience, equipped to take risks in the world. But what sport is there in endangering innocence?'

" 'He brought her to me,' Baldur snapped. 'That gives him a share in her. Tell him his riddle.'

" 'Please,' I said 'no. my head is already spinning. I am not good at word games. Besides, I'm stupid and ugly.'

" 'Yes,' the Persian agreed. 'But never mind. You shall have an easy riddle.'

" 'There are no easy riddles,' I cried. 'I don't want to hear any more.'

" 'Softly, softly,' said the Persian. 'A little uncertainty, a little dismay is always at hand. Why should you escape the general curse just because you are ugly and unhappy? Nonsense. You are alive. With a little trouble, you can learn like the rest of us to kiss and to endure. Now, pay attention!'

" 'I'm a simpleton,' I pleaded.

" 'Never mind,' he said cheerfully. 'You are alive. You have everything you need for hope, for disappointment, for joy. Now, here's your riddle. Listen, once upon a time . . . '

"Abruptly, he stopped. Turning to Baldur he said, 'I almost forgot, prince. There is something you must understand. Because you too are a necromancer, I have given you a riddle suited to your skill. It is no doubt a bit difficult, but it is not beyond you. On the other hand, your brother's riddle is meant only for him. Out of respect for the law of omens, you would do better not to hear what I tell him. Be cautious prince and stop your ears as I tell your brother his riddle or you will confuse the answer to his with the one needed for your own.'

"Baldur shrugged. 'As you like,' he said and put his fingers to his ears. In his lap, the dozing woman began an incoherent whispering. When the Persian turned to me, my heart sank twice—once for fear of his riddle and once because of the Persian's ignorance of my brother Baldur who would cheat when it suited him.

" 'Are you ready?' the old man asked.

"I nodded.

" 'Very well. Listen closely, Fritz. If, once upon a time, the king of an island kingdom that is famous for its horses should, on a Sunday, say of a stallion in the third stall from the left in his stable that it was a goat weighing six hundred pounds . . . Are you following me, boy? . . . '

" 'Weighing six hundred pounds,' I repeated stupidly.

" 'And that it was twelve years old with a long beard and glaring yellow eyes . . . '

" 'Yellow eyes . . . '

" 'And that it needed a nanny to mount . . . are you ready?

" 'A nanny to mount . . . yes . . . I'm ready.'

" 'Then tell me, how would it smell?'

"Again my heart sank twice: once because I could not imagine finding the answer to the riddle, and once because, out of the corner of my eye, I saw that the finger of Baldur's right hand was not in his ear where it belonged but at his temple. So, as I knew he would, my brother had cheated. He knew my riddle and would be sure to solve it before I could.

" 'How would it smell? I said trying to make a show of consideration. 'How *would* it smell? Hmm, hmmm. Horses, stallion, six hundred pounds, glaring eyes, a nanny to mount. Yes, hmmmm. How would it smell?'

"Baldur, pretending that he had only just removed his fingers from his ears asked, 'Are you done, old man? Have you given my brother his riddle?'

" 'Yes. It's finished.'

" 'And you have nothing more to tell us for the sake of this bit of warm meat?'

" 'No,' said the Persian. 'Nothing more.'

"Baldur sniffed, '*My* riddle doesn't seem very substantial.'

" 'Perhaps you are right. On the other hand, it may be that you're wrong. But just in case you find yourself baffled, let me, as a professional courtesy from one necromancer to another, leave you with some clues.' Here, he stepped forward and, in a single easy motion, lifted the sleeping young woman out of my brother's lap. She, still dreaming, pressed her face against the old man's shoulder. 'Now,' the Persian said, 'the clues.' Putting his head back like a bird drinking water at a fountain, he sang in a cracked, melodic voice,

> Send the miller's daughter
> To the moonlit mill.
> Let her stand near water
> That flows beneath the wheel.
>
> Give the girl a fever,
> Let her find out signs.
> Touch her like a lover
> But do not touch her loins.

"With that, and a cheery nod that signified *adieu*, he walked away with the young sleeper squirming in his arms. I saw him bend to kiss her forehead whereupon she quieted at once.

"On the shelf in the cavern where I found her, she had held me close, soothing and winding herself into and around me. Her lips had been in my ear, my hand had followed the curve of her spine and the round of her breast; my tongue had touched her throat. She would have kissed me, I know. She would have curled round and round me in the half-dark while the sounds of other lovers shook the air. On her shelf in that forgotten place, she would have kissed me, but a match flared . . . "

IV

I SHIFTED my weight in the harelip's bed. He believed—he really believed what he said!

And yet he could know nothing about Amalasuntha. As for his prig of a brother, his Baldur—he never got within a thousand miles of her. It was *my* brother Hans who snatched her from the mountain. I had seen him, pale and lustful, throbbing over her, then I fell, smacking my great buttocks against the glass. The miracle of that moment, however, was not that he got her. That was only to be expected. He was Hans, who could arrange the world to suit his pleasure. No. What was miraculous was that from the enclosure of his arms, Amalasuntha managed to send me a look of such tender sympathy that we became—there is no other word for it—we became lovers, sealed in understanding. Two bolts of lightning had crossed a difficult space to pierce and to become each other. I was tumbling, falling, collapsing, and she was being carried away, but before that, the gates of reticence collapsed between us and we exchanged hearts and minds and souls.

Then Hans carried her away while my horse and I slid and pounded down the mountain, whose foot we reached battered but, miraculously, whole. For a while, envy drove me to follow what I thought might be their tracks, but then they were obscured by a deep tule fog and I stopped what would have been in any case a fruitless search.

Here my reverie was interrupted by the harelip, who was saying, "It's strange that, with all of his advantages, my brother Baldur did not get Amalasuntha."

I said crossly, "Of course not."

"He did not get her though he was clever and a cheat besides. The truth is . . . " Here a look of pleasure spread over his face. He seemed for a moment actually to glow. "I hardly know how to tell you . . . it seems incredible, I know . . . but the truth is . . . *I* got Amalasuntha. Oh, I . . . " he made a deprecating gesture. "I don't expect to convince you in the little time we have, but there it is. I'm the one who got her."

I decided not to move or speak. Instead, I would maintain a dignified silence. His tale so far had been a patchwork of overheard conversations, gossip, general information and downright lies. If I made anything resembling a serious response he would take it as a signal that I was ready to accept his invitation for an exchange of stories. My best defense lay in silence. Still, I was uneasy. Though his story was a tissue of unbelievable details, he told it with such vigor that I feared that my own tale, weakened by the paler style of my meditation, might not survive the onslaught of his fictions. Then, shaking my head, I dismissed that as an unworthy thought. Truth was truth. I was who I was. I knew what I knew.

He continued his pleased musing. "Just think how lovely the sentence is, '*I* got Amalasuntha.' What it says is that I, incompetent, harelipped Fritz, rode my horse to the top of the glass mountain; that it was I who bent and lifted the most beautiful woman in the world into my saddle and that it was I who carried her down."

The harelip sounded so reasonable that I found myself nodding along with his phrases. Encouraged, he went on: "I could not help being immodestly thrilled. *I* had triumphed where all the thousands of others had failed. I remember feeling a certain irritation that no provision had been made to celebrate my success. I wanted to preen a little. To strut. To burst into song. I can even recall the melody I wanted to sing. You see" — and here the harelip jumped down from his alcove and actually strutted in the moonlight — "just remembering how I crossed the summit of the glass and the ease with which I bent to take her in my arms restores me to life. I feel my eyes sparkle, my arms turn vigorous, my very fingertips and toes tingle.

"And well they may. It was such a — a lyric triumph. My horse's hooves made a little tune on the glass. His tail whisked at what might have been a fly. It was a warm, sunny day. My muscles moved easily, pleasantly, while my animal, without haste or curiosity, walked on the glass as if it were browsing on a hillside trail.

"On that fine morning I forgot about birds and my mother's monument. It was I, Fritz, split-lipped, dull-witted, lanky and slow who crested the mountain and lifted Amalasuntha into my saddle. Now, wasn't that splendid? Come, come. Admit it."

My heart constricted. I whispered, "Lies, lies, lies. He is a thief of memory, a voyeur of circumstance, a ghoul of other people's experience."

But the harelip, hearing nothing, went on. "Of course you do. I know you do."

Suddenly it was clear to me that we were enemies; that if I was to survive the night to reach Amalasuntha who was waiting for me in that ten-mile square to the north of us, I would have to think against him every minute. If I could preserve my memories clearly, sharply, I would be safe from his torrent of lies, but if I yielded up so much as an inch, I would be lost.

He was just then saying, "Many happy returns of the day. Isn't that what I deserved?" Abruptly, his manner turned vague and uncertain. "Well, never mind. You don't after all, believe me."

"I didn't say that."

"I can hardly blame you. Ugly people have no authority, and I am ugly."

"I'm no beauty either," I said.

"You're right. Still, if you were to tell me your story, I would believe it. Go on. Test me. Tell me anything."

"I've already told you, I prefer not to."

"Well, never mind. So long as you're willing to listen. That's half the battle . . . " He looked feebly around. "I don't know what it is . . . you make me feel . . . formless . . . I find myself telling you things without . . . sequence . . . without order. I don't mind your thinking me mad, but not disorderly. My mother would not have liked that. She had a rage for order."

"Your mother?" I said. "Is she part of your story?"

"Of course. Long before Amalasuntha and her mountain, there had to be my mother. There had to be a kingdom and my mother's birds. There had to be chickadees, cuckoos, flamingos, nighthawks, snowy owls, eagles, goshawks, honey buzzards, plovers. There had to be wrens, merlins, crested coots, cormorants, pigeons and storks. There had to be . . . "

"Birds," I said. "I take it you mean birds."

"Yes," he agreed sadly. "Above all, there had to be birds."

V

"BIRDS, birds," he muttered, wrapping himself in a trance. His eyes closed as words flowed from him in a steady crooning hum. Tall and ugly, with a split lip and twisted features, he seemed to be singing against the dark hoping for some trick of nature to make an echo that would prove the existence of his words. I thought of a dark shore on which he might be singing; of a forest in which he would utter himself to leaves and branches as he cocked his ear, waiting for another voice as hushed and eager as his own to make a reply.

I knew what he was doing: He was speaking to me. I was that other voice hidden in the forest or in the spaces between the waves of the sea. He was waiting for a cry as inarticulate as his own and he was hoping it would come from me. I understood his temptation. How often in the last ten years have I strained my voice and ears in just that way without ever hearing a whisper in reply as I, now, did not reply. Tomorrow, Amalasuntha would be in my arms, ending my need for such vexed songs. I had only to wait the night out. When I left the tower in the morning, I would find her in the ten-mile square to the north. She could be nowhere else for I had looked.

"Birds," the harelip was saying. "Birds in a thick question mark across the sky. A mother who might have loved me." In the moonlight, he looked like an underwater statue lost from a shipwreck pale and floating.

The harelip peered across the space between us. "Have I mentioned my father to you?"

"No."

"Probably not. I did not really know him either. He died when I was two years old and he was thirty. His portrait shows a commanding figure with a thick beard, gray eyes and a strong right hand grasping the hilt of a sword while he stood in a pose of readiness. You would have said that *Be Prepared!* was his motto. He had all the chivalric skills. He could joust, wrestle, sing, play on a harp, ride and hunt.

"He *looked* like a man whose destiny it was to be the emperor of the world. All his life, he waited for the call to a great occasion. Alert, erect, his eyes unclouded, brave, he was ready for dragons, giants, trolls, but wherever he looked in his actual kingdom he saw barley fields, sheep or mules. Minotaurs never roared before his portcullis; cyclops did not haunt his mountains and he never heard the tramping feet of invading armies marching through his domain though he wore a fresh uniform every day.

"Still, he achieved distinction of a sort. He died in my mother's arms at the very moment he was conceiving my brother Baldur. In a love-making that my mother would later characterize as typically indifferent, he startled her by popping his eyes and uttering a brave martial cry. Then he gave something like a leap after which he fell and died on her breast. 'Gone,' she said, 'gone away like a puff of smoke in the breeze.'

"What a ridiculous way to become a widow." Hesitantly, the harelip asked, "Do you find widows especially interesting?"

I thought of my own mother who was also a widow. I thought of her vapors, her chills, and her vast collection of hand-embroidered handkerchiefs. I remembered the suspicious vitality she showed in the old Persian's proximity and I lied. "No. Not especially."

"They are, you know. In the folklore of many countries, widows are the absolute emblems of female loneliness and experience. If they are young and beautiful they are actually believed to give off an erotic effluvia that makes them irresistible to men though I must say that that was not characteristic of my own mother who . . . who . . . " Here a look of puzzlement darkened his face. "Oh please," he said, jumping down from his window alcove, "if you have any skill with the written word, won't you help me? I have a document. Something my mother left . . . or seems to have left me. It is all very ambiguous. I find it hard to believe she wrote it, and yet, there is some evidence to suggest she did . . . . Perhaps you have some discernment in such matters."

"I can read."

"Good. Oh, good." He came closer still and said, "May I sit beside you?"

"It's your bed," I replied.

He sat, if the truth be told, uncomfortably close. I could feel the knotted muscles in his shoulders pressing against my arm. He smiled one of his loose-mouthed smiles at me as if we were co-conspirators. "What makes it hard for me to read this—what shall I call it—day-book of hers is that I am her son. I can't trust my own judgment, you see, and I need help. Because I want to be fair." He averted his eyes as he began to search his rags. He looked for a moment like a man frantically scratching himself. "Ah," he sighed, "yes. There, I have it."

He held up a roll of scorched leather. "It's as if she knew I would want to set the record straight. She was such an orderly woman."

I said, "Is there something there that you want me to read?"

"Oh yes. Very much. I hope the smoke has not spoiled it. It was stupid to burn the aviaries."

"You burned—aviaries?"

"My brother's idea. Still, I must admit I didn't stop him. I'm willing to take my share of the blame." He shook his head. "It isn't that I wasn't glad to see them burn, you understand. It's only that it wasn't my idea."

I said, "There's something there you want me to read?"

"Oh yes. Of course." He waved his roll of parchment at me. "Read it, but don't hold the burning of the aviaries against me. It wasn't as cruel as it sounds. Only a few thousand of the birds died. Several million others got away."

He shuddered. "Birds are stupid, you know. Feed them and they love you. However warm their feathers make them appear on the outside, the truth is, that deep within they are reptiles. There's never been a bird you could kiss or cuddle without getting your face scratched. Greedy, greedy things. Utterly unlovable."

"Perhaps," I said. "If you want me to read whatever that is, you'll have to give it to me."

"Yes. Oh yes." Suddenly he knelt and for a moment I was afraid he was going to kiss my foot, but no, he unrolled the parchment packet and put the loose end in my lap. He spent an unnecessary moment smoothing it out for me, then he went back to his alcove where he sat with his back against the stone. The moonlight streamed in behind him.

I picked up the end of the parchment and found that, in order to ready anything, I had to tilt it almost entirely on its side to let the moonlight spill on the handwriting. The script was so small, so neat and round—and yet so hesitant, that I needed every particle of illumination I could get.

The handwriting proved to be utterly charming, even touching, as if it were made by a schoolgirl who had nothing but her penmanship to be proud of. Neatness, restrained impatience, loneliness spoke from the thin shoulders of her letter m's and the hesitant curve of the dashes which appeared sparingly on the beautifully lined pages. The letter i was so modestly dotless, the periods at the ends of sentences so self-abnegatingly light that my heart was wrung. What talented and exiled young creature had written these words? In what tiny cave of her soul did the writer of these lines live that she could shape such diffident c's and d's. Even as I studied her l's and p's, I could not help thinking that if Amalasuntha were not irrevocably in my thoughts, I might find myself falling in love with the shy woman whose soul was reflected in this noble calligraphy.

Someone intricate and, at heart, beautiful had written these words. As I held the smoke-stained pages to the moonlight, I read:

Entry 2684

I must be a trying mother. On the other hand, the boys are trying too.

Entry 2685

When I look into Baldur's eyes or catch a glimpse of his face, my heart freezes. Hidden in his eyes, there is an accusing knowledge that he knows some dreadful secret, and whatever it is, it strikes me with fear.

And then there is Fritz who persists in tilting his ruined face up, waiting for a kiss that not even a less fastidious mother than I could give. What have I done to deserve these two?

Entry 2686

My poor owls. Wet, naked, sick . . .

Entry 2687

Fritz had no business teasing the bird. A split lip is no excuse. At that age, the owl is homely too. He ought to have had some fellow feeling for the little thing.

Entry 2688

My husband! My prince of majesties. I fitted in his arms, but did I love him? "Come, come, come," I cried with a fine show of exaltation. "Come, come come," and then he shuddered; there was a flash of light, a surge of heat, and a great weight of inert flesh fell on me. Clay cold. Moist, immovable and already turning rigid between my thighs.

I pushed him off. I was not panicked. Women are given such tasks, and so I did it. I pushed my husband's weight aside and stumbled to the bedroom door where I called, "Help, help." Still moist from our lovemaking, and the seed of our next child already in my womb, I had to stand in the drafty doorway crying, "Help, doctor. Help, chambermaid."

When the doctor came, he looked suspiciously from the corpse to me. "What happened?"

"I killed him," I said, pulling my robe closer around me.
The doctor studied the body, turned it over, peered into the clay mouth, prodded the place between its legs and shook his head. "Amazing," he said.

"I killed him," I moaned.

"I'm afraid so," the doctor agreed, but his voice had already taken on a lewd inflection. "He died a glorious death, Madame."

I stood beside the body of my husband, too weak to show myself offended. Instead, I asked, "Of what did he die?"

The doctor smirked, "A surfeit of delight, Madame."

Entry 2689

Baldur says that he and I are co-murderers, having killed his father together. I was the entrapping vessel, he says, and he the venom. He makes a grisly kind of sense, but I wish he would keep his subtleties to himself. How can I love him? Co-conspirators do not love.

Entry 2690

Birds utter their melodious cries. They fly. They own the sky. They swoop and dive. Their short, swift breaths, their rapidly beating blood keep time to their songs. They have neat, firm beaks.

Entry 2691

Baldur's gray eyes indict me. Fritz has no look in his face except a grimace. Birds, except for the ostrich, the dodo and the chicken, are inevitably graceful.

Entry 2691

The ruddy-duck when first hatched is a downy, gawking creature. When it has learned to swim, it cleaves the water in a catenary arc, a mathematically elegant curve.

Entry 2693

Yesterday Fritz turned his unorganized face up to me. "How may I serve you, Madame?" he asked. He is a feckless boy who keeps risking the rejections that he earns. I put my dissecting knife down and said, "You could try growing a mustache." Baldur, who was swinging in a hanging chair and heard the exchange, decided to chide me. Not for any love he has for Fritz, but rather for the pleasure he has in showing me his contempt. "Mother," he said, "that was very cruel."

"How would you suggest I treat a boy whose features don't hold still?" I replied.

"You might try kissing him" he said. I knew that, as he spoke, he was laughing up his sleeve.

Entry 2694

The shrill music of the birds of prey. To my ear there is something decidedly flutelike about a hawk's cry as it poises in midair before it swoops. A notable point: After hawks have mated, they fall silent.

Entry 2696

Fritz, who is incapable of tact, has written me a note. It says, "Dear Mother, I love you? In our forest there is a catalpa tree with widely spreading branches, but it is white and naked. Stripped of its bark and leaves, it stands like the idea of a catalpa tree in the mind of a man who tired of thinking about trees. It is without a wound to show what killed it. Deep underground, the taproots know what vital juice is missing from the soil."

The foolish boy. Does he think I could miss what he no doubt thinks is the killing irony of the question mark at the end of the first sentence?

Entry 2697

Fritz is at it again. He has slipped a clipping from the *Royal Journal of Ornithology* under my door. If he thinks I will crumple with guilt, he is sadly mistaken.

The clipping:

The mother cackling goose lines the nest with feathers plucked from her own breast, selecting only the warm down closest to her skin. In a winter of extreme severity, after a heavy snowfall, it is not unusual to find her frozen body still sitting on the eggs she would not abandon to the mercy of the snow.

VI

I WAS roused by the harelip's moist cough. I folded the parchment of his mother's journal and waited for him to come and take it from me. He stood immobile for a while, then he stepped down from his alcove and crossed the space between us. "What do you think?" he asked as he took the smoke-stained parchment packet from me. "Is it genuine?"

Behind him, at the edge of the horizon, the moon glistened like a gilt barrelhead. It cast its light over his shoulders, making him look like a huge stalagmite growing up from a limestone cave. "In what sense genuine?" I asked. "The parchment is real enough. Ten or twelve years old I would say."

"That may be. It isn't the parchment I care about. I want to know whether my mother's expressions of love are real."

"There is no expression of love. The word is a single reference, more or less in passing in your mother's text."

"What about the story of the cackling goose who dies caring for her young? Surely that should count."

"That's in a note that Fritz slipped under your mother's door."

"I'm Fritz. Much good it did me." He stood, caressing the packet. Back in his alcove, he settled himself against the stone and said, "Isn't it strange how the written word *feels* like proof. It has authority, doesn't it? The word on the page . . . so immovable, so inexorable.

"I have, for example, another document." He began a second search of his rags. "Ah . . . here . . . no . . . no . . . there, I have it." He waved a card at me. Even from across the room, I could see that it was an ordinary postcard which showed a young woman reclining beneath a flowering catalpa tree. The shimmering moonlight and the distance between us kept me from knowing whether she was naked or not.

"There," the harelip said, "you are a man of discernment. What can you make of this?"

"Can you tell me," I asked, "whether the girl on the card is beautiful? At this distance it's hard to tell."

"It's just as hard for me. The ink is very old. Had I been the writer, I would have sent a much shorter card."

"Are you going to read it?"

"You really want me to?"

"I think you want to."

"You *are* discerning. Very well then. Here goes." In a hasty, rasping voice, he read:

Dear Klaus,

   I am much disordered since I saw you last. Would you believe that I have turned fearful. The aloof competence that you admired has been shaken and I no longer look out at the world with imperturbable eyes.

   How could you know what I know? You will say that you are my brother; that you have fraternal sympathy. Nonsense. I am no one's brother. I was not born.

   I came into the world fully grown, riding my black charger across a plain spread out under a night of burned-out stars.

It was autumn. I passed watch-fires of green wood where men bent and coughed as they waited for someone to sing.

I came into your world as one who passes through, riding from shadow to shadow past soldiers and the women they chased. I heard their skirts fly up; their breathing as they were dragged into thorn bushes. I heard tittering, sobbing and the sound of flesh being thrust against military drums, then the low resonance as young men reached and plunged and fell away.

Always, it was contemptible. I expected nothing more. For me, two eyes would always be too many for this world.

I heard an owl call me by name. I would have ridden on, but I passed under the owl's high tree and heard it saying, "You." The owl said, "You." Looking up I saw a woman hanging from a branch. I took my dagger and hacked the rope that held her. Once, twice and then she fell. She lay where she had fallen, her eyes blinking. She or the owl said, "You."

Why is it that everything is so disordered? As if I were fat and innocent, like you?

From the beginning, I had more memories than if I had lived a thousand years. I ride now, as always, upon a world that is a dying cinder. If I could do more harm than I have, I would.

Fat brother, Klaus, where are you?

Hans.

VII

THE harelip stopped reading. His mouth continued to move, however, as if he were summoning up enough spit to ease a dryness. He cleared his throat and would have said something except that he sneezed. A spaniel's wispy, silly little sneeze that distracted my attention. For a while he busied himself with his sleeve and his nose. Then he said, "Well, how do you like that for a postcard? Interesting, eh? Especially if you happen to have a brother named Hans who doesn't, may I say in passing, sound like such an appetizing character."

"It's a matter of indifference to me what you say." I hated the rudeness in my voice, but it seemed important for me to keep him at a distance. No familiarity, that had to be my rule. As for the postcard, of course it was unsettling. In every way it might have been written by my brother Hans. On the other hand, how was one to know? It was not like him to be 'disordered.' Even his contempt, which sounded authentically like Hans, was muted. I said, "I wonder if you'd let me see the card?"

He ignored the question and said, "Tell me, do you think it's genuine?"

"What would that mean? There must be many men named Hans."

"Who have fat brothers named Klaus?"

"Yes, even that." My cool replies disconcerted him. He sat hunched forward in his alcove, his heavy shoulders slumped, his thin thighs and legs drawn up to his chest, looking so much like a dying spider that I had a twinge of remorse. What, after all, would be so wrong if I offered him a little comfort. Why not join him in whatever exchange of miseries would ease his pain? I felt my tongue nerving itself for speech and I might even have spoken except that his harsh voice intruded. "All right," he said. "Let's put the card down as one more failure. Instead, let me tell you about my mother and her birds. You already know something from her parchment scroll, but there is more . . . "

I must have nodded because he smiled his gaping smile and launched immediately into another of his monologues. This time I ignored him though I let him talk. I sat quietly, calming myself after the shock his postcard had given me. Then, because I wanted not to be invaded by his words, I closed my mind against them and set myself to remembering the Persian and his visit to our country.

VIII

THE Persian arrived in our capital during the summer of our worst drought, carrying a pack at whose tip there perched a monkey. Behind him walked a saffron-stained young woman whose beauty her dusty blouse and ragged skirt did nothing to obscure. From one end of a yoke across her shoulders there hung a covered cage; from the other, a saffron grinder's mortar.

The old man was tired, but his movements were charged with energy. At the marketplace near the fountain he went to work. Within minutes, a glittering yellow tent with green and red pennons flying from it swayed in the hot breeze.

When the tent was in order, the Persian created a small stage of planks on which he set the covered cage, then he reached into a bag from which he took a pair of small cymbals which he handed to his ape. At once, the creature set up a weary banging while the Persian stood, his arms folded across his chest, ignoring the racket as he watched the crowd forming slowly around the tent. When there were some hundred farmers and shopkeepers and market women standing before him, the old man put his arms out as if he were offering a blessing.

"This is the place!" he called. His accent made the language of my country seem exotic. "This is the place. I have arrived . . . . I bring you news from the darkness that

you fear. I bring you hints and guesses, portents and signs."
There was a movement in the crowd. The Persian, to offset
the disturbance, raised his voice. "Friends. Listen. Are you
afraid to die? Then gather round. Are you afraid to live?
Then come close; come closer.

"Oh, my friends. Are you tormented or miserable or
poor? Are you powerful, happy and rich? Ah friends,
whichever you are, the future lurks like a tiger just around
the turn of the road. It waits like a throne on which you
may sit; it yawns like an abyss into which you may fall.

"Step up, friends. Step up . . . . I bring you news.
Come close and hear! The future is a mystery but Tetragrammaton, the Creator, condescends to send you clues.
Tetragrammaton, the Holy Name, the Unshattered Vessel
of Light, and the Keeper of Darkness permits you to
make shrewd guesses. The Loving Source of Our Being
has loosened the sutures of his skull to let the light
shine through. Microprosoppus, his other Self, who makes
the patterns of the stars and shapes the motions of the
planets . . . Microprosoppus Himself writes messages my
bird will find.

"Come close, come closer. Step up. That's it, my
friends. Offer your pence, your rupiyahs. God writes
straight with crooked lines. Step up and buy."

The old man tilted his head back like a drinking bird
and sang:

> Is there blood in your stool?
> Does your meat taste like dung?
> Is your husband too old?
> Is your mistress too young?

> Are your teeth falling out?
> Is the going too rough?
> Let me help you to find
> When enough is enough.
>
> Buy portents, buy portents,
> Come buy, come buy.

The crowd watched as he moved, kicking one foot out and then another as if he were a marionette whose strings were snarled. He chanted:

> God wants you to know
> Without telling you so . . .
> It's His little joke
> To hide sparks in the smoke.
>
> Buy portents, buy portents,
> Come buy, come buy.

He stopped to wipe the sweat from his forehead. The monkey, unmindful of the heat or the crowd, kept up his clinking. The entire scene—the Persian, his girl, his ape and the crowd—shimmered as if it were fixed in gelatin.

Then the Persian heard the splash of the marketplace fountain and roused himself. Turning from the spectators, he went to the cage and plucked away its cloth cover to reveal a white cockatoo that stood blinking at the sudden light. While the bird clung to its perch and preened its feathers, the old man went to the fountain where he filled a cup that he carried to the cage. He pressed a latch and the cage door fell open. He reached the cup to the bird which bent to scoop the water into its bill in quick sideways motions after which it threw its head back and let the liquid slide down its throat. The monkey on its platform stopped making its racket and crouched, scratching forlornly at its fleas.

The crowd was entranced. The antics of the monkey had been interesting, and the Persian's mélange of mystery and doggerel amusing, but neither the man nor the monkey were unique. The cockatoo was. In my country, no such bird had ever been seen. The people were pleased. How neat and white the bird was; how jaunty and crested. How cleverly it drank.

My brother Hans and I were there on horseback, breathing the sun-scorched and dusty air, enduring the flies and the stink of urine in the marketplace. We were out for the afternoon, looking for relief from my mother's pallor, from the scented languor of her undiagnosed illness. When she did not have fever, she had chills. When these relented, migraines invaded her head. And always she turned upon us her bleak, victim's gaze, as if to say, "All this that I endure, I endure because of you." Naturally, whenever we could, we found occasions to be out of her sight.

We were riding through the market square when Hans noticed the Persian's booth. Heavy as I am, I would have been just as glad to keep riding, hoping to find a tree in whose shade I might take refuge from the sun. But Hans, my strong-willed brother, made us stop.

The cockatoo in its cage continued to drink. When it was done, it flicked its beak fastidiously, then stepped and fluttered to the door of its cage, looked about briskly, hopped out, looked about again as if measuring the crowd and then, in a whir of wings, it flew to the top of its cage where it perched. A thick-set butcher with black curly hair and beard, his thumbs tucked into strings of his bloody apron, called out, "Hey old man. Is it a singing bird?"

"No, the bird does not sing."

The butcher waved the flies from his apron and tried whistling toward the cockatoo, but the notes he made came out muffled, flat. His failure puzzled him. "Can it talk?" he called. Can your bird talk?" The bird, as if choosing to answer for itself, emitted a dry *grrrrrrrkkk*. The tension in the crowd broke. There was laughter and a general movement closer to the booth.

The Persian's pretty follower stepped out from behind the makeshift stage and set a stool beside the crouching monkey. On this, she placed a stone bowl into which she poured a handful of crocus stamens. Seating herself cross-legged before the stool, she went to work pounding the saffron whose sale, I presumed, augmented whatever money the Persian earned with his prophecies. From where Hans and I sat astride our sweating horses, the old man and his entourage made a rather pleasing picture. The tall Persian, the strain of exhortation ebbing from his face, the saffron-stained young woman bent over her bowl, and the scruffy ape taken together looked quaintly . . . how shall I put it? . . . comfortable. One had the sense that they had been at home together in many places.

The butcher, bothered by the flies and angered by the failure of his whistling, pushed through the crowd toward the mountebank. "Hey, old man," he called, "is your yellow-stained girl for sale?"

"I sell clues, hints, signs. You look a lively young fellow with, no doubt, a remarkable future. Step up, young man."

Putting a hand to his bottom, the butcher replied, "You know what you can do with your omens, old man. But I am a judge of meat. That yellow-stained grinder there looks sweet and tender. Sell her to me."

"She is not mine to sell. She is awake. Speak to her yourself."

The young woman at the pestle smiled. The butcher, conscious that he was now at the center of the crowd's interest, drew himself up. "Hey girl," he bawled. "What do you say? Will you belong to me?" The cockatoo, at the tip of his cage, clucked."

"Come on," the butcher coaxed. "What good is the old man to you? Lamb is a daintier dish than goat."

The saffron grinder stood and looked first at the butcher, then at the Persian. As we watched, we saw her eyes darken. Then, her youth and the Persian's age, as if there were a song between them, flowed together, quickening them both. There was a long interval in which she seemed to be holding her breath. Then, as if reluctant to take her eyes from the Persian, she turned to the butcher. "Yes, meat," she said, "meat is your highest wisdom. But what else do you know? As for him," she indicated the old man, "I can *see* him. But you," and here her hand went to the back of her neck where it sought a damp curl which she twisted for a moment as she went slowly toward him, "though I smell the blood on your apron and I hear your voice, try as I will, I can't see where you are." She passed her hands into the air as if she were blindly searching. "You are there, somewhere. A young, bloody nothing." With the merest hint of switching hips, she returned to the stool, before which she knelt and resumed her interrupted task. Hans, behind me, gave a nearly inaudible "Whew!"

The Persian poked his ape and it resumed its chiming clatter as the old man called, "To business, to business my friends. The future is dark, the present confused, and the past is a thread of regret. Step up and buy! Step up and buy my tokens, my hints, my signs." As he talked, his fingers were busy. From an oblong, red-lacquered box that appeared in his hands, he now pulled a number of cards, which he tucked into the ribs of the cockatoo's cage. The bird fluttered down into the dust and began to whet its beak against the stone.

There was a sudden *craaaack* and a pebble careened off the saffron grinder's bowl. At the sound, the bird fluttered into the air, flapped its wings, then dropped back into the dust where it settled, its head toward the butcher who, still swaying from the violence with which he had thrown the pebble, stood, an isolated figure in front of the crowd. "So much for you and your signs, old man."

The Persian, checking first that the young woman, his ape and his bird were unhurt, turned to the butcher to whom he said mildly, "Yes, I am old and you are young. My hair is white and yours is black. Still, I will share a secret with you."

"No, no," the butcher drew back. "I'm buying none of your portents and signs."

"Never mind, young man. What I have to say will cost you nothing."

"Free, eh?"

"Yes, free. Because you are so young. And I am so old."

"If it's free, than I don't mind. Prophesy away."

"Then listen:

> Whoever you are,
> Whatever you do,
> Whatever your star
> Or whoever you woo;
>
> If you have a bold
> Or a cowardly eye,
> If you don't get old,
> Young man, you will die.

The crowd, delighted to see the butcher discomfited, roared with laughter. The butcher hitched up his bloody apron and swaggered back into the crowd where he was soon lost. The Persian, when he had turned the cage into what looked like a beehive studded with white cards, rose to his feet and called, "Now, friends, we are ready. The future, like a shy bride, anxious to be glimpsed by her groom, waits. For a small coin, I will pull back the eternal curtain. Now, who will be the first to buy?"

The cockatoo left off whetting its beak and, with its wings outspread, moved like a dowager with full skirts as it circled the card-studded cage. I heard a deep sigh behind me and turned. My brother Hans was leaning forward in his saddle. "All right, old man," he said. His lips were tight; his eyes narrow. "Let your bird find me a token."

A look of hesitation crossed the magician's face as he saw my brother and me. First, he bowed, to acknowledge our royalty, then speaking to Hans he said, "Your Highness, my bird and I are mere servants of chance. We stumble . . . we wander . . . we are often confused. We know nothing certainly."

"Yes," Hans said coldly, his voice cutting through the heat. Sitting erect and pale on his black horse, he was an imposing figure. "Yes. You've said all that. Now, turn your bird loose for me."

"Reconsider, prince," the Persian begged. "A glance at my rags will tell you that my bird and I do not always please."

"What do I care for your rags? Get moving, old man. Turn loose your bird."

The Persian hesitated. Facing the crowd, he put his arms out as if pleading for sympathy. "Citizens . . . friends . . . I sell hints, signals and signs. I offer riddles and guesses. My bird is in no way supernatural. It is a foolish bird that does not sing or talk. When I am given a coin, it hops about cocking its head at the tickets I have stuck around its cage. It hops. It opens and closes its eyes. At some moment, moved by the sheerest whim, it stops and snaps up a card in its beak. There is no secret here. No hidden corn by which the bird is guided; no thin silver wire attached to its legs. My sleeves . . . see . . . " He hastened to roll them up. "My sleeves, as you see, are empty."

"Catch!" snapped Hans, and there was a sudden arc of silver in the air made by the coin my brother had thrown. The Persian, with the dexterity of long practice, reached an arm up and caught the coin then looked down sadly at it in his palm. "It is a large coin, prince," he said. "My needs are small and you are altogether too generous. You are already a prince. Perhaps you will let my bird choose a card for someone else."

Hans, in a voice like knives being sharpened, said, "The coin is mine. Let the card be mine. Turn loose your bird for me."

The old man frowned. The heat of the late afternoon seemed to be gathered in his narrow shoulders. "Prince," he began again, "the days that are to come come unannounced. It may be wisdom to ignore the shape of their coming. Besides, you are a prince. You are already at the top of Fortune's Wheel. Enjoy the present undisturbed."

I, sitting heavily on my horse, had my eye on the saffron vendor who, enraptured, was watching my brother Hans. He was so tall, so well-mounted, so slender, so gracefully made. The look on her face made me feel twice as heavy as I already was. I felt the sweat coursing into every fold of my skin.

Hans, oblivious for the moment of everyone but the Persian said, "Peddler, you bird is wiser than you. It says 'Grrk.' I have thrown you a silver coin. You sell portents, signs and tokens. Sell me mine." With his head thrust forward, Hans looked just then like the figure-head of a particularly dangerous warship. The saffron vendor, as if she were thirsty, sucked air through her parted lips. From the crowd there rose the acrid effluvium that people give off when they are hoping to see violence.

The heat congealed us all and for a few seconds, we simply stood there as in a tableau. Then an unseen child wailed and an unseen father struck her. There was a ripple of protest from a bystander, then a reply. Someone said, "I'll break you in two." "You and who else?" came the retort. A breeze fluttered the Persian's rags. I could see the blue veins on the back of his hand, like traceries on a parchment map. My brother had his hand on his dagger.

"Grrrrrrrrk," said the cockatoo, and at the sound the crowd let its breath out. The scuffling over the slapped child stopped and there was laughter. The saffron grinder smiled. Hans, controlling himself, said, "Well!"

The Persian bowed. "Very well, prince. Because you command it, my bird will choose for you." He clicked his tongue and the bird started off, moving with a dainty side-to-side swagger. Round and round the ticket-studded cage it went. Sometimes it walked; sometimes it hopped from one foot to another. Sometimes it made brief flights through the air, flying so low that its wings dragged. Hans waited. The saffron vendor watched him closely, and I watched her.

Round went the bird. Round and round again. Though it kept to its circling path, its movements were erratic. Then there was a flutter, a squawk, and it was suddenly hopping a little way away from the cage with a bit of pasteboard in its beak. The Persian called, "Here, now!" and the bird flew to his wrist, adjusting itself on his thin bones, where, with the card in its beak, it rocked as if it were having trouble keeping its balance. Then, with the same motion it had made earlier when it was drinking, it tilted its head back, holding the card up to the Persian who took it.

The Persian looked down at the card and I thought at first, "Maybe he doesn't know how to read." Then, as he continued to keep his eyes riveted to the bit of pasteboard in his hand, I thought, "Perhaps whatever is written there is in a language he cannot understand."

"Well?" said Hans, his hand once more on the hilt of his dagger.

"Prince," replied the Persian, "my bird and I are . . . stumblers. We are agents, not principals. We are nothing.

We are not to be blamed. You paid for the card itself. It is yours."

"Stop babbling and give it to me."

"Yes, since it belongs to you," the old man said. He held the card out and Hans took it. For the longest time, he stared down at the bit of pasteboard and I wondered again if he had forgotten how to read or if he was reading a language he could not understand.

Hans's horse, sensing something ominous from the sudden rigidity of its master's body, curvetted once and would have reared but Hans's hand on the bridle aborted the movement and brought the animal to a quivering standstill. For the interval of a heartbeat, man and horse seemed carved in bronze, then Hans called, "Old man, be careful. Toy with fate if you like, but do not toy with me. You will find me dangerous." With that, he dismounted from his horse in a single, graceful motion and, parting the panic-stricken crowd with an imperious gesture of his hand, he moved toward the saffron grinder. As he passed me, I saw a droplet of blood on his lower lip where he had bitten it.

"Prince," the Persian said, stepping forward as if to bar Hans's way. "Prince, the woman is innocent," but Hans was already past him, his right arm outstretched.

"Hans," I groaned as I dismounted from my horse and followed him. "Hans, whatever is written on the card, she did not give it to you. Wait." Oh, I knew my brother and how, with a touch, he could reduce a woman to pliant clay. Whatever he was about to do, it would be passionate and cold.

By the time I had waddled fifty steps, he was already doing it. His right arm was around her and he held her, actually restraining her for the moment from pressing herself against him. I felt my bowels churning when I caught the look of eagerness in her eyes. "Hans," I called, but the dust and the heat turned me giddy and I stumbled and fell with a great thump. I lay, more or less rocking on my great stomach and I pleaded again, "Hans, oh Hans, leave her alone."

But the truth is, I was not interested in saving her. Sick of my innocence, what I really wanted was to have her for myself. I wanted my right arm to be around her the way Hans's was. And I wanted to do what he then did: He put his left hand into her blouse and I could see the motion under the cloth as his hand moved over what I imagined was the most beautiful breast in the world. "Hans," I pleaded. "Leave her alone." And what I did not cry was "Hans, you spoiler. You have always had whatever you wanted, why this time, won't you leave her for me?"

The devoted look in her eyes, her dry thirsting lips, the near lunge with which she pressed herself against him when he finally kissed her made me wail. I could smell her heat and its sweet acrid odor clotted by blood. I knew where her belly was that instant and what her loins were doing even as Hans's cruel lips and hands touched her.

When it was clear to the Persian, when it was clear to the crowd that he could turn her, move her, wind her and bind her at his will and she was gasping uncontrollably in his arms, Hans let her drop. Licking the speck of blood from his lower lip, he turned and walked back to his horse and mounted. To the Persian, he said, "You have your warning, old man." Then, with a twist of his left hand, he turned his horse's head and rode off at a canter.

I lay in the dust, red-faced and fat and ashamed, still clawing at the air. In the shimmering heat of the afternoon, the saffron grinder shivered and, using both hands, drew the edges of her disordered blouse together. The Persian draped a shawl over her shoulders and said, "Come. We must move on." With that, he busied himself putting his pack together. He folded the tent and its pennons, tied the planks together and stowed them. He returned the cockatoo to its cage, then he gathered up the tickets with which he had studded it and returned them to their lacquered box. When his pack was once more on his shoulders, his ape climbed the old man like a tree and took its place at its tip.

It was then that the old man came over to me where I lay in the dust like a cockchafer skewered on a pin, waving my arms and legs feebly as I tried to reach the offending card my brother had dropped. The old man knelt and pushed it toward me, saying, "Here, prince. See what your brother saw. Farewell."

I clasped the card between my fingers and peered at it. Then, fearing that I had it wrong-side up I turned it over. Try as I could, on first one side of the card and then the other, I found nothing at all to read. Nothing.

Still bearing the blank card between my fingers, I staggered finally to my horse and mounted. As I rode slowly out of the square, the butcher called, "Meat. That's what it is. It's all meat." His mirthless cackle followed me until, at the bend in the road leading to our castle, it abruptly stopped.

IX

FRITZ'S voice, sounding like pebbles grinding on a sloping beach, intruded on my reverie. "I feel much better now," he said. "In fact, I feel perfectly well." He stood up in his alcove, flexed his arms, snapped his fingers and rolled his shoulders in a display of exuberance.

"Good," I said, meaning to sound perfunctory but he took the very fact of my reply as a sign of enthusiasm.

"How kind you are. No, no," he said hurriedly when I made a denying motion with my hand. "Would you like to hear the story of an encounter between me and one of my mother's baby owls?"

It was the last thing in the world I wanted to hear. Actually, I longed just then for solitude. I wanted leisure in which I might sit and hear my memories humming like a spinning wheel: memories of the Persian, his ape and cockatoo; of my mother and Hans; of myself and the saffron grinder. Above all, I longed for quiet in which to recreate and savor the miraculous exchange of glances that took place later between me and Amalasuntha. That glance in which we recognized our love, and in which she conveyed to me the whole story of her life. No, I was anything but eager to hear this harelip's gravelly voice grinding in my ear.

But, as my mother used to say, "If you cannot be nice,

you can at least be civil." So I was polite and said, "You have a story about an owl?"

"Oh yes," Fritz said eagerly. "And you want to hear it?"

"If you like."

"And you will listen?"

"Yes."

"Oh how good you are."

"Please," I could not help saying, "don't be fulsome."

"No, no. Of course not. Now, to the owl . . ." He looked down at his hands. "Hmm. Hmm. I wonder," he said shyly. "Have I told you that my mother was a tiny woman — very fat and full of a charging energy?"

"No," I said. "You did not."

"Well she was. A small, fat woman. The thin feet of a hummingbird perched on her forefinger could make it seem like a sausage bound in wire. Her eyes were brown and piercing. Do you know something?"

"What?"

"She was . . . how shall I say it . . . it's hard . . . it's not the sort of thing a son can talk about easily . . . but my mother was . . . well, she was generously endowed as to . . . bosom. When I think how lonely she made me feel and then remember the warmth that I occasionally sensed emanating from her breast, I get confused. Do you think . . . is it actually possible that she might have rocked me to sleep on her breast? Or brushed my torn lip with a loving finger? Tell me. . . . you are a man of experience. . . . is it possible?"

For a moment, I thought of my mother's handkerchiefs and her migraines, then I said, "Possible? Of course it's possible."

"I see what you mean," Fritz said. "It's possible in an abstract sort of way. But not in the real life I knew. There, it can't have been true. She was so speedy, always dashing past me on an important errand to her aviaries.

"Baldur, who, from the moment he was born, never had any illusions about her, used to say, 'Fritz, the odds were against us from the beginning. Think: We weren't hatched from eggs. We don't have beaks or feathers or wings. Between sons and birds, there is a mighty difference.'

"But Baldur hated her always without forgiveness. My heart was softer. I was always ready to lift my face in her direction; and I never stopped dreaming of kisses.

"You must understand how truly engrossed she was in her work with the birds. Even at night, even in her bedroom, she had time to minister to them. There was always an ailing bird in a cage on her bedside table. Sometimes a hawk, sometimes a finch. Once, even, an austere flamingo.

"On the night I'm telling your about, I woke to the sound of the wind whooshing slowly through the rafters of my room making a sound like whispers whose meaning, if I could only pay proper attention, it seemed to me I might grasp. So I listened closely and, in a little while, I thought I understood, though what the words were, I cannot, to this day, be sure.

"In any event, I got out of bed and went, barefoot, over the cold stones in the long corridor that led to my mother's bedroom. When I got there, the room was utterly dark except for a candle that shed a warm glow over a cage on my mother's bedside table. I crept closer, wondering which new bird was receiving her attention now. I climbed into her empty bed and, crouching on all fours, I peered into the cage where there was a young horned owl afflicted with a disease with a name so long that I can no longer remember it.

"The owl, in fact, was very unwell. Its murderous feet kept only a tenuous grip on its soiled wooden perch. It was a young bird and had not yet lost all of its yellowish baby down. Whatever ailed it had produced bare patches on its breast and throat, and I could see its reptilian skin fluttering over its ragged pulse.

"You know, my mother had millions of birds. She had eighteen thousand seven hundred and ninety-one owls alone. And yet, she had time to care for this one.

"Oh, how I envied that owl. I tried, by looking into its eyes and studying the quality of scaly skin on its legs and the various tints of its feathers to learn what it was that had made my mother choose this bird for her care. And what it was that I had failed to do. There must, I thought, be something essential. If I could only discover that essence; if I could only imitate, or be infected with it, I too might be hung in a cage and cared for.

"I crept closer to the cage and, putting my face next to the bars, I said, 'Hoo.'

"The baby owl had been hatched in a protected darkness. Broad-faced, fierce-beaked parents had coddled and guarded it. They had flown around it, haunting the night with their thrilling cries. They had fluffed their feathers in preparation for flight and had gone off in search of wood-rats, pocket mice, spotted skunks and bats with which to feed it. They had flapped their wings and hissed at intruders so that this little creature now leaning drunkenly on the perch in my mother's bedside cage might grow in its turn into a night bird like themselves, capable of wheeling into a clear evening sky as it hunted small animals.

"It would have done all that, except that one of my mother's emissaries, wearing a stout leather glove and a wire mask to protect his eyes, found his way to the place where the owls had their nest and extracted this infant from it, despite the clicking beaks and furious wings of its parents. He had removed this owl and borne it away to set it before my mother who, from the moment it came into her hands, loved it.

"I leaned forward and stared. The pulse under the bald patch in the owl's throat beat quickly, but the bird kept its eyes closed. I hooted again. This time, I put my whole soul into the cry. When nothing happened, I tried again, working to perfect my call. There was no response except the fluttering of the tiny pulse in its throat.

" 'It's dreaming,' I told myself. 'It's dreaming of its descendants; of the legions of horned owls yet to come; of its mother . . . her clicking beak, her ruffling feathers. It's dreaming of its father, with his yellow eye and saber claws.' Overcome by tenderness, I put my finger into the cage, meaning to pet this repulsive creature that my mother loved. To acquire, perhaps, by touching it, some of its amazing luck.

"Before my finger could reach the owl, there was a sound like a bubble of air rising out of porridge. The bird straightened up on its perch. Its beak opened. Under the bald patch where its pulse had fluttered, there was now a slow rolling motion, as if mud were being stirred there. I smelled the sour odor of fish and wet feathers. The owl's beak widened, its eyes opened and it returned my gaze just as it let a moist ball of fur and bone slide upward from its stomach to its throat, then into its mouth from which it rolled down through its opened beak to fall to the bottom of the cage.

"You may be sure I was bitter. Before that round moist faceless bit of debris could happen, my mother had had to feed meat juices and tidbits to her owl. She had pounded meadow mice and gophers, flying squirrels and killdeer into pastes that would tempt it's appetite. Now, because of her affection, it would recover.

"Then I was angry. There rose, in my own gorge, a tight ball of feeling. I was in my mother's forbidden bedroom on my knees inside her empty bed. I put my thumb to my nose and waggled my fingers at the owl as I tried to put contempt into the hoot I was about to make. Hard as it was to purse my torn lips, I said, 'Hoo.'

"The owl, roused from its lethargy by my cry, snapped its eyes shut and then opened them again. Sick as it was, it puffed its feathers, then, arrogant with the full consciousness of its superiority, turned its broad face to look directly at me and hissed."

X

THE harelipped Fritz's voice faded. "A childhood confrontation," he said. "Bested by an owl in pin-feathers."

Even across the distance that separated us, I could see that his skin had turned the color of blue clay. "Please," I said, "try to calm yourself. You don't look any too well."

"As well as may be expected. Still, if you don't mind, I'd like to finish my story."

"I'm sorry. I thought you had finished. Go on." Beneath me, in the bed, something surged and rolled. If there were vermin in it, they must be huge.

"An owl in pin-feathers," Fritz resumed. "After it had dropped the ball of its digested victim and hissed at me, I lay, waiting for tears to come that would wash me away in a stream of salt water. What came instead was my small, energetic and fat mother who had her attendants carry me out of her room."

To stop the harelip's flow of speech, I murmured, "You've had bad luck."

"I have, haven't I?" he said eagerly, as if my faintly sympathetic phrase were a gesture of friendship. "You'd think I might have won a competition against a half-dead owl."

I was tempted to smile, but, given his pathetic hunger for affection, to smile in his presence seemed a dangerous gesture, so I forbore. Actually, what I most wanted to do was to shut out the sound of his voice so I could return to my memories, so that, in my mind's eye, I could watch the events that followed on the Persian's first appearance in the marketplace of our capital city.

I closed my eyes and recalled again how Hans, after he kissed the saffron vendor, had ridden away and left me holding a bit of blank pasteboard in my hand. The crowd had melted; the Persian, carrying his pack on which his ape was perched, had left the market square, followed by the saffron vendor who, on a yoke across her shoulders, carried the cockatoo's cage and her grinding equipment. Some minutes after they were gone, I mounted my horse and rode in their direction. At the turn in the road that leads to our castle, I thought I caught a glimpse of them.

Still clutching the blank card in my hand, I shouted, "Hey, Persian. Wait. I need you." He seemed to wave an arm acknowledging my cry, but in the next instant he disappeared beneath the crest of a low rise.

I will never know what it was that prompted me then to dismount from my horse to follow them on foot. I think I did not want to seem proud when, finally, I should catch up with them. Or I did not want the saffron vendor to think of me as in any way like my brother Hans. Whatever my reason, it was, for a man of my bulk, and in that heat, an absurd decision.

Not many minutes after I began to walk, I felt my underwear chafing my loins. My riding boots, too, were no help on the cobbled highway. And yet, for another half hour, I continued my punishing walk. Finally, I gave up and turned off the road and crossed a ditch into a field in which there was a large oak tree, in whose cool shade I took refuge.

I had just settled myself with my back against the oak's broad trunk and was beginning to feel some relief in its shade when, out of the corner of my eye, I caught a glimpse of something moving, like a sudden display of white feathers in a lady's fan. Then the patch of white flickered again. Despite my fatigue, I rose and followed the movement into the nearby woods. I heard a twig snap, and then, right before me, there was the cockatoo, displaying its tail. Slowly, I went toward it where it stood on a dead branch that stuck out from a log. The thought came to me that if I could catch the bird, I might be able to squeeze from its whiteness some clue as to the meaning of the blank card I carried in my fist.

The cockatoo cocked its head to look at me and waited, unafraid. Then, when I was almost on it, it rose into the air and made a brief flight to a low branch of a pine tree where it perched expectantly. Again I went toward it; again, just as I was nearly upon it, it made with its tail feathers a noise like a drum muffled in a blanket and it was off to a new resting place, this time on a moss-grown hummock of earth.

I followed and it fled, leading me always deeper and deeper into the wood. The rustle of its wings merged with the whisper of the leaves of the trees among which we moved. Finally, it alighted on an old tree trunk where it stood, flirting its tail as if to say, "Here, young fool. Catch me now. This is the place." I took a deep breath and, heavy as I am, I lunged toward the bird.

The clatter of my stumbling sent the cockatoo into the branches of a catalpa tree in the very center of a sun-filled clearing into which, after my fall, I rolled. The cockatoo looked down indifferently at me and preened its feathers. Exhausted though I was, I got to my feet and started toward it once more. Then, some uncanny sound made me pause. It was a sere, insistent rustling, as if desiccated bees were humming in their hive deep in a hollow of the catalpa tree. It was an ominous sound which, I felt, was meant to warn me—of something, but then the cockatoo uttered a jaunty cluck and I plunged ahead, determined to get my hands on him.

I stumbled again and nearly fell on the sleeping saffron vendor, who lay curled beside a log inside a vee of sunlight formed by the shadows of a couple of thick branches of the catalpa tree. The log was old and covered with bright green moss that served as a bed for a profusion of scarlet poppies over which, in scintillating motion, there hovered a cloud of tiger butterflies. With her flushed face, and her slightly swollen lips, the saffron vendor had the replete look of an infant who has just finished nursing. Her blouse was open and looked as if it had been lately disarranged.

I stared. Then I heard the dry chirring that came from the catalpa. I reached down and touched the sleeping woman's face. The warmth of her skin passed into my fingers and went from there, in a great surge, right to my heart. As if the passage of that warmth were a signal, the timbre of the noise in the glade began to change. What had been a dry chirring as of shrunken bees sounded now like the high humming of gnats; that sound, in turn, changed to an insistent and shrill chirping, like cicadas taking to the air. And under all these sounds, there was another, low and insistent, that seemed tantalizingly close to human speech, though the only word that I could catch sounded like "No."

My first impulse was to flee and it's what I would have done to avoid being soiled. But her warmth was already in me. And now I could smell the fragrance that rose from the folds in her clothing: a compound of saffron and sunlight. So, frightened as I was, I passionately desired to do what I was about to do.

First, I tucked my brother's blank card into the pocket of my breeches. Then I whispered, "Go away, bird." But the cockatoo merely cocked its head and continued its indifferent swaying on its branch of the catalpa. "Well," I thought, "let it be a witness. Who will believe a bird that speaks no language anyone can understand."

With as much care as my great weight permitted, I got down on my hands and knees and crawled slowly through the warm grass toward the saffron vendor. Then, my mouth was open and I readied my tongue for the sweet salt taste of her sweat. And I might have tasted it, too, if I had not just then noticed the ant.

It was walking across her bare shoulder, waving its feelers in all directions, hesitating, circling. It was an ordinary ant, as innocent as myself and it moved without intent back and forth over her shoulder. Suddenly it veered and headed down into the tiny hollow of her collar bone where, for a while, as if confused by her perfume, it scurried about in circles after which it moved down the line of her throat and into the cleft between her breasts.

What was I to do? There was the ant, scurrying into a place where my eyes had not dared to look. The sight of that impudence intensified my desire. The ant, as if it knew what it was doing, started up the exposed round of her right breast. It paused at the delicate brown aureole, then moved slowly, tentatively around it. God is my witness, though I meant what I intended to do, I was frightened beyond any clear thought of what that might be. I knew only that her fragrant warmth in the sunlight had made me dizzy. And that I was tired. I remember thinking that I ought to run, but I was already on my knees watching the circling ant. I felt the blood in my veins turn gritty and then the part between my legs that I had been taught never to touch *began to sing*. To sing. It hummed and thrummed; it surged and sang.

What happened then can hardly be called my fault. I felt my blood turn to honey as the ant, hurrying more quickly, moved in ever-narrowing circles. At any moment, now, it would climb the sleeping woman's rosy nipple. She, for her part, as if she were responding to the movement of the tiny legs, stirred and breathed more quickly. A single drop of moisture gathered at her lower lip and I found myself staring into it.

The ant ran round and round. Inside the crystalline droplet of moisture on her lip I could see her image, as one sees a reflection in a clear pool. There, she was on her knees, cupping a newly-budded flower; but even as I watched, that image changed and now I saw her bending over snow-covered stones in a frozen brook leaning forward to scratch a name with her finger on a sheet of ice.

The ant, as if frenzied, circled her breast. Still on all fours, I crouched beside her, then, like a heavy bear, I rose to my knees. Slowly, I opened my doublet. Cautiously, tenderly, I pushed a lock of her dark hair away from her temple, then I pressed my cheek to hers. I think the silent glade itself heard my sigh as I placed my body beside hers.

So close. So close that I could feel the beating of her heart as it pumped the blood which, with the help of sunlight, warmed her skin.

With my right arm around her, I let the forefinger of my left hand follow the ant which was on her nipple now. As my finger, just barely touching it, learned its outline, I felt her nipple swell.

I took my hand away and watched the ant which, now that it was at a summit, seemed not to know where else to go. As for me, I think I held my breath. I know I waited as if time were all the membrane between me and happiness. And then the ant made a movement so taunting that I fell upon it and put its life out with my tongue.

I cannot, or I refuse, to remember all that happened next, though it is true that at some point I had her in my arms and at another I did something violent with my breeches so that I might lend myself into her flesh. She stirred; her breath, like the smell of fresh-cut apricots, filled my nostrils. Then, in the deepest part of the swoon into which I must have sunk, I felt a slap against my naked buttocks.

When I floated up into the light of the sun, I found myself looking into the Persian's eyes. His ape was on his right shoulder and was peering quizzically at me. The saffron vendor, her blouse fully unbuttoned, was sitting up, rubbing her eyes. The acid taste of the ant on my tongue was proof that whatever had happened had not all been a dream.

"Well, prince?" the Persian said.

I turned my face away.

"Well, prince?"

"I didn't do anything," I said. "I killed an ant. That's all."

"Then why do you tremble? he asked, putting one bony arm around my shoulder while, with the other, he helped me pull my breeches back up.

"Because she frightened me."

"No. You frightened yourself."

"Button her," I pleaded. "Please."

He put his hand on her shoulder and she adjusted her blouse. "She did not mean to tempt you. She was asleep." The woman yawned and stretched and scratched the back of her head. "You were asleep, weren't you?"

With the flat of her palm, she rubbed her blouse over the place where I had killed the ant. "I was asleep," she said. "You know I was."

"Of course you were."

"Go home," said the Persian as he helped me to my feet.

"No," I said stubbornly. "No. I want . . . I want . . . "

"Yes, you do. Like all of us. But now, go home." He whistled, and the cockatoo flew down from its branch in the catalpa tree and perched on his left shoulder.

"I have no horse," I protested, but even as I spoke, there came my white horse sauntering around the moss- and poppy-covered log, sending the tiger-butterflies into the air with a flick of its tail.

The Persian's arm was strong as steel as he pushed me up and into my saddle. "Go along, prince. Go home."

I turned my horse's head and rode to the bend in the road that leads to our castle. By then, the taste of the ant in my mouth was almost gone.

XI

I was just letting my mind drift to the next occasion on which I saw the Persian and his entourage. It was an altogether complicated episode and would have required careful remembering which I could not just then undertake because the harelip chose that moment to cross the space between his alcove and the bed on which I sat. I was so engrossed in my thoughts that I might not have noticed him standing before me if it had not been that, as he came toward me, he blocked for an instant the shaft of moonlight that illuminated the tower room. The flicker of darkness he made brought me rudely back to reality.

"You know," he said, putting his hand under my chin, "silence is the easiest form of evasion."

I pushed his hand away and said, "It is also a fence to wisdom."

"A fence includes . . . "

"And it excludes."

"Oh, stop your clever prattle." He looked weary. "See me. Hear me. And stop your infernal hiding."

"I'm not hiding. I'm waiting."

"So am I," he chided, "and yet I talk to you."

"I wish I could give you what you want." Then—how can I explain this—I began to tremble. The man was beyond my understanding or care, and yet my heart contracted at the sight of his resignation. He, mistaking my tremor for something else, said, "You're cold, poor man. Here, take back your cloak." Suiting the action to the word, he laid my cloak in my lap.

I almost, almost, succumbed. The thought came to me that, after all, we were the only two living creatures in this desert sector of the globe. Why would it be wrong to respond to him? Then I took a grip on myself. "Careful," I cautioned. "The claws of pity are still claws. Another such spasm of fellow feeling and I may end by losing Amalasuntha. Let me once join him in his tale-telling and who knows what tricks he will use to shake my confidence. Oh no. My story is true for only so long as I can guard it with silence."

And so, though I said, "Yes, thanks," and pulled my cloak up to my throat like a blanket, I hardened my heart and kept my counsel. He, when I said nothing more, turned and went back to his alcove while I closed my eyes so I could hear Amalasuntha's voice repeating, in a secret cranny of my brain, the story of her life that I received in its entirety when we looked into each other's eyes just as I fell on the slope of the glass mountain and my brother Hans was bearing her away.

XI

THAT long look of Amalasuntha's distilled itself and became the syllables of her sweet speech.

"From the beginning, there was my father. And, as I grew, the distant murmur of the forest. His words mingled with the creaking of trees, and the sound of brooks spilling over stones. And the voices of courtiers and even my mother's voice, though how I heard her I really do not know. Voices. Sounds. A medley of syllables and tones. Whispers, words, naming me, naming my father . . .

"He was a well-made king. Twenty-eight years old, clear-eyed and alert, he could, in his dress uniform, seem a commanding figure, an admirable man who had the rosy glow of dawn in his smooth cheeks and a passionately vacant look in his large dark eyes.

"In the room where my mother bore me, he raged around her bed. " 'Liar,' he shouted. 'Cheat. You promised me a son. What shall I do with this squalling creature with its cleft?'

" 'Whatever you like, my lord,' she was still able to say. Loyal to the end, had she had strength enough, she would have clasped him to her breast.

" 'Whatever *I* like. *I* like,' he growled, chewing at the yellowed corner of his drooping black mustache. He was very close to tears. My tiny, gaping mouth, from which there came repeated wails of hunger, frightened him. The birth and death processes repelled him. Here, before his eyes, the great fluxes were taking place. His wife was dying and, in a room that smelled of blood and feces, of soap and mother's milk, there was, in a basket at her bedside, a scarlet infant with the clay-blue paste of birth still on it, kicking and gasping, making demands. His gorge rose. There was altogether too much wet detail in the room. It was no place for a king whose natural habitat was on a throne, or astride a charger pursuing deer through the royal forest trails.

"The soft silt of death was already darkening my mother's eyes, but my father continued to shout, 'You fraud, is this the meaning of your promises?' My mother, who was already wandering in mists that only she could see made no reply. 'You promised me a son,' he raged. 'Look at this . . . this . . . Is this a son? Well, is it?'

"My mother did not reply. A simple fisherman's youngest daughter, she had never expected to be a queen until that fateful day when my father, ill-disguised as a country gentleman, paused to eavesdrop on her and her sisters where they sat watching the waves shatter on the breakwater that guarded the bay from which their father sailed early every morning.

"It was actually the oldest sister who first saw, and recognized, my father standing in the shadow of a boulder. At twenty-eight, he was notorious as the most eligible bachelor in the kingdom. For more than a decade, he had resisted every match proposed for him by his counselors. But lately, after it had been made plain to him that his people were not willing to be governed much longer by a wifeless monarch, he had agreed to marry, reserving to himself, however, the choice of his bride.

"Now, here he was, hidden in the shadow of a boulder, eavesdropping on the conversation of the three daughters of a fisherman who were, after the oldest sister's signal, entirely aware of him and who he was.

"'Oh sisters,' the eldest daughter said, raising her voice to make sure it would reach the king who was leaning forward, a hand at his ear. 'Do you know what I would do if I were queen?'

"'No,' replied her sisters. 'What would you do?'

"'I would go to the Witch of the Wood and ask her to teach me the Art of Cooking for a Queen, so that I might reach the king's heart by delighting his palate."

"'Oh,' said the second sister, 'that is no doubt a worthy ambition. But I . . .' And here she cast an arch look in the direction of my father's boulder.

"'Yes, what would *you* do?' the other two sisters asked.

"'I, too, would go to the Witch of the Wood so that she might teach me the Arts of Love, with special emphasis on the Seven Hundred Ecstasies from Head to Toe so that I might delight the king each night in our bed.' She giggled, and made a great show of hiding her blushes.

"'And you, little simpleton, what would you do if you were the queen?' Here the two older sisters turned to my mother.

"If she was a simpleton, her sisters soon had reason to envy her maladresse. 'I,' she said brusquely, 'I would give the king a son.'

"It was then that my ill-disguised father stepped from the shadow of the rock beside which he was hiding. Taking my mother by the hand, he said, 'You will be my queen,' and to his courtiers, who were in hiding beside their rocks not far away, he called, 'My search is over. Blow the trumpets, ring the bells.'

"That is how my mother outwitted her envious sisters and left the foggy village and the smell of fish to become the queen of our country.

"For nine months all was well. There were silks and satins, diamonds and pearls. Rare foods, fine wines and the extravagant obedience of many servants. She basked, also, in the glow of her sisters' envy and her father's pride. What she had not counted on, what she had not even thought about in the moment when she uttered her wisdom, was that the chance that a queen — any queen — would give birth to a son was one in two.

"At the end of nine months, there she was, the exhausted mother of a girl, listening to my father bawling curses at her while I, my head twisted in a rage, squirmed and writhed and howled. Not many minutes later she was dead.

"As for me, I was alive and avid and dark and thin. My hair, wet and plastered close to my skull, was long and black. I smelled of the slime through which I had come. When my father no longer had my mother to shout at, he turned to vent his rage at me but, looking down, he caught sight simultaneously of my cleft and my as yet untied cord. Unnerved, he fled the room."

XIII

LIKE chalk grating on a blackboard, there came the harelip's voice breaking into Amalasuntha's tale. "I wonder," he said, "if one of my dreams would interest you."

"Haven't you already told me one? 'Bested by an owl in pin feathers.' I think that's what you said."

"No, no, no," he hastened to say. "That was no dream. That actually happened. What I want to tell you now is a dream I dreamed when I was a child. Then I'll tell you how my mother's monument came to be built."

"That was after you burned the aviaries?"

"Yes, but remember, that was Baldur's idea, not mine, though it is true that I helped him.

"He was always an enigmatic boy, full of slippery intelligence. He was tall, lithe, agile and had the sensual look of a faun. His eyes were gray, his mouth soft, his skin smooth. His mirror, unlike mine, was always his friend.

"He showed considerable skill as a necromancer, even as a child, though it is true that, when we were very young, his talents were generally squandered on projects to bedevil me. For instance, he would wait until I had come to a particularly exciting part of a book I was reading and then, reciting one of his formulas, he would turn into asterisks all the words on the pages to come. On another occasion, he cast a spell over my horse so that for a little while it was able to talk. But, since Baldur's spell was not powerful enough to endow the beast with intelligence, all I got from that experiment was a couple of hours of unilluminating conversation with my horse about hay and oats; and a certain uneasiness about mounting him later when the spell wore off.

"Of course I minded his mischief, but I took it as the condition of my life. I was ugly and clumsy, and he was handsome and gifted. The contempt with which he treated me seemed only natural. So I was all the more surprised when I came down with a tertian fever to find him in a dream engaged in a quarrel with my mother on my behalf. My mother, as always, was hurrying to the aviaries where, this time, she meant to provide nesting materials for a colony of Great Auks, but Baldur stopped her. He caught her by the sleeve and said, 'Fritz is sick, mother. Very sick.'

" 'Shamming,' she said and would have gone on, but he would not let go of her sleeve. I, in my bed and enclosed in a membrane of heat, took pleasure in watching them. If they could quarrel about me, my split lip and my ugliness counted for something after all.

" 'No,' said Baldur. 'All you have to do is touch his forehead. He's burning up.'

" 'Nonsense. He has a simple indisposition which a few minutes' flight in the morning air will cure. The young coot's temperature can vary . . . '

" 'Mother! Fritz is not a coot.' There was no trace of anger in his voice, but he was regarding her steadily.

" 'I know better than anyone what he is. A self-pitying, ugly creature. Clean his perch and put a bowl of fish broth inside his cage. That'll set him right.'

" 'Your *son* has a tertian fever.'

" 'Shamming, shamming, shamming,' she said briskly.

" 'Dying,' Baldur replied. 'Dying.'

" 'Don't be absurd,' and she tore her sleeve out of his grasp.

" 'Will you look at him or not?' he demanded. I, in my bed, watching them, was proud of his anger in my service.

" 'Out of my way,' my mother insisted.

" 'No,' said Baldur. 'Wait.'

" 'I must go. I'm late,' And off she started, in her diminutive, bustling way.

" 'Wait,' Baldur urged. 'Wait.'

" 'Out of my way.'

"He stepped aside but before she had gone three paces, he said, 'Alright. But remember, you brought this on yourself, mother.' With that, he pointed the forefinger of his right hand at her and said:

> *Kanti, kantil kleros . . .*
> *Jah, Shamgaz, Istemah,*
> *Merigaz, Merigaz, Merigaz.*

"I felt my fever subside even as the pain in my throat increased. Then I saw my mother moving slowly, as if the air around her had thickened. Slowly and more slowly she moved until she came to a stop. Then there began a transformation that started at the top of her head and then descended to touch her neck, her shoulders, her breast, her waist, her hips, her knees, her legs, her feet.

"At first, though I saw feathers appearing where her hair had been, I did not fully understand what was happening. But by the time the change had reached her waist I could already recognize the turkey buzzard into which she was turning.

"Baldur continued to chant and suddenly the transformation was complete. The turkey buzzard lifted one scaly leg and flexed its gray claws. Through the window of the room in which I lay, there floated the bright trill of a nightingale who, I felt certain, was perched on one of the slender branches of the great cedar tree in our garden.

"At first, the song of the nightingale seemed to refresh the air in my bedroom, but then the turkey buzzard opened its beak, gaping, and the music-filled breeze was driven back to the garden from which it came. Now, the thick odor of ill-digested snakes, of rotted turtles and meadow mice filled the room. I stirred in my bed, wanting to warn . . . somebody, but the phlegm in my throat impeded any sound I tried to make.

"My mother, now a turkey buzzard, adjusted her wings as if they were heavy and hunched forward, putting one foot carefully forward, then another. She moved, swaying a little from side to side, teetering, balancing. Her small head gleamed in the light of the candle on the table beside my bed. The feathers around her neck were bluish black, and her body plumage a dull, cottony brown. The candle flickered, making Baldur's shadow tremble on the wall. The turkey buzzard, her curved bird's feet unused to marble floors, moved uncertainly toward him.

"'*Amerlai?*' Baldur stammered. It was a question spoken by a frightened boy and not the self-confident Baldur I knew. '*Amerlai?*' Something was wrong.

Out in the garden, the nightingale, who was not part

of this drama, continued to sing on its thin branch of the cedar tree.

"When the turkey buzzard was directly in front of Baldur it raised a reptilian claw with which it plucked at Baldur's doublet. My brother made no move to avoid the claws. He stood still while the bird tore open first his doublet, then his shirt. When his chest was exposed, the turkey buzzard uttered a complacent *Khhhhhhhhhh*, and thrust its head forward. With its dull, curved beak, it first nipped, then tore at his flesh, pulling away layers of skin and muscle, making a three-inch incision from which no blood flowed.

"Again, the bird's head struck. I heard its beak grind against bone, then there was the sound of a crack and the wound in Baldur's chest grew perceptibly wider. Baldur stood, his hands at his sides, and waited, showing no sign of pain. The buzzard took a step back, cocked its head and studied the gash it had made in Baldur's chest. It saw what I from my bed could see, the gleaming red of Baldur's pulsating heart. Then, its eyes gleaming, it thrust its parted beak forward and snatched the heart out of Baldur's chest.

"At first, all I noticed was that the song of the nightingale had come to an abrupt stop. Baldur stood immobile, as before, and watched while the turkey buzzard, her son's heart still in her beak, began to tear feathers from her breast with a claw. I smelled newly plucked feathers, then fresh blood as the bird cut a gash in its chest. There was what felt like a long interval while the turkey buzzard stood on one leg, holding Baldur's heart with its other claw and its own heart in its beak. I heard a cry as Baldur and the turkey buzzard swayed together but I could not be sure whether it came from Baldur or the bird. Stiffly, the buzzard hopped toward Baldur while he leaned toward it. When they were only a foot or two apart, the buzzard set its own pulsating heart into Baldur's open chest. In a nearly graceful, bowing movement, it then put Baldur's heart into the empty cavity in its breast. Each time the bird completed a movement, Baldur winced.

"The exchange was made and the two stood for a while like creatures woven into the border of a tapestry. Finally, Baldur trembled and raised his hand to cover his wound as if he were ashamed. The turkey buzzard proudly smoothed the feathers that covered the gash in its chest.

"In her own voice, and in her own shape, my mother said, 'I don't like your tricks, my boy. I think you will live to regret them. Now, out of my way.'

"And, for a wonder, my brother moved. When she was gone, Baldur stared down at his chest where, now, there was only his uninjured doublet, all scarlet and gold. Shaking his head, he came to my bedside where he put his hand to the pulse in my throat. 'Fool, fool, fool,' he whispered as he worked to bring my temperature down. 'Fool, fool.' Which of us he meant, I did not know.

"An hour later, thanks to Baldur's ministrations, my fever subsided and I sank into a deep sleep. But that did not happen until after Baldur bent over me and I got to hear the beating of whatever heart it was that was now in his chest. The very last thing I heard before I slept was the nightingale indignantly resuming its interrupted song."

XIV

"SURELY," I told the harelip, "that was a dream."

"I said it was, and I think it was, but how can I be sure? One thing is clear, Baldur never forgave my mother for that exchange of hearts as I know from what happened after she died."

"You mean the burning of the aviaries?"

"That fascinates you, doesn't it? That was merely arson, a kind of house-cleaning after she died. No. What I'm talking about is my mother's monument."

"You built her a monument? How touching."

"Wait," the harelip said. "You may not think so. You see," and here he resumed the slightly forward-leaning stance which by now I recognized as his tale-telling posture, "my mother died not long after the turkey-buzzard episode with Baldur. A tiny scratch on the little finger of her left hand poisoned her blood and killed her before she had a chance to put her research journals or her diaries in order.

"There was something very melancholy about the field in which we buried her—it had been a polo ground that belonged to a cavalry *caserne* that had been abandoned long ago. Why Baldur insisted on putting her there, I don't remember, unless it was the nearly perfect flatness of the ground over which the wind blew steadily from the east. On warm days, one could still get whiffs of ancient manure from the nearby ruined stables and watch flights of starlings pecking in the dry soil for seeds.

How quickly my mother's grave was lost in that unrelieved flatness. On the day of her burial, there was a low mound over it, but a day or so later, the soil itself had so shrunk and hardened that there were no visible signs that a woman, much less a queen, was lying there. Had polo players returned to the field, they could have played even a furious game without disturbing the footing of their horses.

"When Baldur suggested a monument for my mother, I, who was still haunted by what I had seen or dreamed in my sickroom, was suspicious. 'Why would *you* want to build her a monument?' I asked.

" 'She was my mother too,' he said. 'I owe her something.'

" 'What?'

" 'Respect. Honor. Filial piety.'

" 'Hmm,' I considered. 'What sort of monument? Marble, granite, steel?'

" 'Too typical,' he said, and I saw at once that he was right. 'Pertinent! That's the key. Appropriate. Specific. Something that lets the world know at a glance her essential essence. Nothing banal, nothing ambiguous.'

"My heart sank. Here was my brother Baldur once again thinking ambitiously, imaginatively. Whereas I would have set a small marble stone on her grave carved with a legend like, *Here Lies Mother*, Baldur's mind grappled with essences. 'No,' I stammered. 'Nothing ambiguous. Characteristic, of course.'

" 'Precisely. And what, dear brother, most characterized our mother's life? What was her predominant passion, her most cherished joy?'

" 'Birds,' I said. 'Birds.'

" 'Aha!' He slapped me on the shoulder. 'I see that your head is more than a resting place for your cap. Good thinking. Now, Fritz, suppose . . . '

"I should have known right then and there that he was not to be trusted. But praise is an irresistible elixir. That slap on the back, that 'Good thinking' rendered me utterly pliable.

" 'Suppose,' he was saying, 'suppose the birds them-selves were to build her monument.'

" 'The birds?'

" 'Yes. Think of it. Suppose the birds she loved—I mean *all* the birds, everywhere. Suppose they flew over her grave, and suppose each bird plucked a single feather from its breast and let it fall. Think of it. Millions and millions of birds; millions and millions of feathers falling over her grave. Then imagine those feathers linked by the power of my spells, forming an airy tower rising toward the sun.'

"I felt the worm of suspicion trying to turn in my brain. Cautiously, I said, 'You want that? You want that, for our mother?'

" 'I do,' he said piously. 'I do. Yes, Fritz. Think of it, a feathery mountain, all grace, all elegance and made indestructible by my spells. A multi-colored, lofty, shim-mering . . . '

" 'You can do that?'

"He smiled. 'It won't be easy, but with your help, yes . . . I can do that.'

" 'My help. I know nothing about spells and incantations.'

" 'Leave the magic to me. But you'll have plenty to do. There'll be a pentacle to dig and catalpa cuttings to gather.'

"There was indeed plenty for me to do. For the next three weeks, I was in the polo field every day working with pick and shovel, digging the five-sided trench that Baldur's spells required. Each of the ten sides of the pentacle needed to be 180 yards long and I had to set catalpa cuttings at eighteen-yard intervals along each side. Moreover, I had to choose the cuttings with care, since no sprig could have more than eighteen leaves on it, or less than twelve. It was hot, hard work, but as the sweat ran down my sides and I tasted the dust in my mouth, I knew that I was laboring in a holy cause.

"Baldur, as I worked, sat on a canvas chair and studied his book of spells. From time to time, he looked up and waved a hand to encourage me.

"At the end of the third week, I was wakened an hour before dawn by Baldur's whisper, 'Get up. Wash, but don't eat or drink.'

"I did as I was told. Seven minutes later, after a brisk gallop, we were at the polo ground. In the light of the false dawn, the sprigs of catalpa I had set out looked lonely.

"We dismounted and tethered our horses several hundred yards away from the pentacle, then we made our way toward it. When I glanced at Baldur, I could see that his mouth was set in a grimace. He held his book of spells so tightly against his chest that his knuckles showed white. Something, a blood vessel or a nerve, made his left eyelid flutter.

"Off in the ruined stables the starlings were chirping sleepily. In the warm wash of the spring breeze, we could detect a current of icy air. Overhead, the stars were fading.

"Baldur positioned me at the apex of the triangle to the northeast. When the birds come,' he said, 'say nothing. Watch the grave. Watch the birds, but say and do nothing. If you get scared, close your eyes. No matter what happens, don't move or speak. Is that clear?' I nodded solemnly. He turned and walked across the field and took his place at the apex of the northwest triangle.

"Our mother's grave was in the geometric center of the ten-sided figure I had constructed. According to Baldur, the pentacle, viewed from any direction, can be seen as a schematic diagram of a human figure with a head, outstretched arms, and spread legs. If his spells worked, the birds he summoned would approach the pentacle from the south, entering it between the southeastern and southwestern points. They would circle the grave once, then each bird would drop a feather and fly out of the pentacle, going back the way that it had come, but at a lower altitude.

"I stood very still and watched my brother. He seemed taller than I had ever seen him. Holding the book of spells in both hands, he pointed it eastward, in my direction, and recited an incantation in a voice that seemed to chime like a glass that has been struck by a silver knife. I pressed my hands together, but it seemed blasphemous just then to pray.

"Baldur rocked back and forth. Across the distance between us, there came snatches of his incantation, ' . . . and the supernal H, *Heh* encloses the spirit. It is the fifth letter. It is the aspirate out of the lungs of the Creator of All Things.'

"'Oh, H, oh *Heh*. Oh aspirate. Oh spirit of the winds, blow. Oh H, oh *Heh*, blow, blow, blow. By virtue of the supernal blow, blow. By virtue of his all-seeing eyes, blow. Blow heron, horn-bill, hummingbird, hawk. Blow. Blow.'

"He paused. For a while, he stood calmly, untroubled and in command. Then in a distant barley field a cicada chirped.

"The noise of the cicada startled him. He looked about uncertainly, then bent to his book again. 'By the letter H, blow. By *Heh* and by *Huh*; by H, by horses, by hounds, blow, blow. By *Heh*, by *Huh*; by *Huh*, by *Heh*, blow, blow, blow, blow.' His voice cracked; his face twisted toward the newly risen sun. He took a deep breath and cleared his throat. When next he spoke, his voice was preternaturally deep: 'IN THE NAME OF THE SKULL OF BGVLGTHA; IN THE NAME OF THE BALANCE OF BONE AND AIR, blow through the hollow bones. BLOW!'

"He stopped. Far away, in the foothills of our country, lambs frisked and goats butted heads near blossoming cherry and apple orchards. The starlings in the ruined stables were already busy with their lechery. A rooster with a voice like a fish-hook tearing silk crowed. The sun spilled through a gash in the clouds. The first insects, with the daylight now on their backs, began to rustle in the grass. Somewhere a cow stumbling toward its drinking trough moaned. Off in the castle, the servants dragged themselves through their morning duties. It was dawn, the hour of regret, of anticipation, of renewed desire.

"Baldur stood at his point on the pentacle. His face looked like a daytime moon, luminous but indistinct. If the spell he had recited was meant to bring the birds, his luck, so far, was bad. Even the nearby starlings in the stables ignored him.

"Baldur turned again to his book. This time, he spoke earnestly, slowly, intimately, as if to a friend he was trying to persuade. Around him, as the morning air turned warmer, there was now a gathering of intensity. He spoke, or prayed, or pleaded for a long time and his speech was filled with many pauses.

"As I watched I felt a change in the air. The sun, the dissipating clouds, the sprigs of catalpa bordering the pentacle, all seemed to waver, as if I were looking at them through a lens held by a trembling hand. It was then, in a middle place fifteen degrees above the horizon and at the same time beneath the sky, that I saw the Garden.

"It was immense. There were myriads of flowers in meadows, on lawns, in orchards. There were rivulets and pools and brooks from which deer drank.

"But the chief wonder of the place was the size and the number of its trees. And on every bough of those millions of trees, there perched birds of every kind, each bird swaying on its branch, singing or waiting to sing. In the denser boughs there were nests and the air around those trees was cheerful with the noisy comings and goings of parent birds tending their young.

"Baldur's prayers rattled in my ear. I realized with a twinge of pity that he could not see the paradise on which I gazed, but that did not prevent his voice from invading it. His words plucked at the membrane of perfection in which the Garden was enclosed. He swayed back and forth, like a tottering statue. Lifting his head, he stared straight into the sun as he cried,

The source is one
And the current is two
And the basin breaks into seven.

One and two and seven are ten,
Blow through the hollow birds.

"There was a silence, then the clear membrane that enclosed the Garden tore.

"The birds stopped their rustling as, from a tree in the center of the Garden there rose a single chickadee. It veered uncertainly, then mounted higher and higher until it hung in the air, its wings canted, after which it twitched, turned and started in our direction. An instant after the chickadee had left its branch, a bewildered cuckoo followed it. After the cuckoo, there was a flamingo which was followed in turn by a nighthawk with a gaping bill. One by one, a number of tiny birds followed whose names I did not know but whose flight made a thin dotted line across the heavens as the birds flew toward the pentacle.

"For a while, I watched the ascent of bird after bird without allowing myself to admit what had happened. It was only when a horned owl broke out of the Garden on its muffled wings that I faced the truth: Baldur had succeeded. The birds of the creation were climbing the sky to do his bidding. Our mother was going to have her monument.

"The birds came on: a royal eagle, then a dapple-breasted goshawk; a honey buzzard, a golden plover; a lapwing, a curlew. A crow and a stork joined those already in the air. Then a lark, a wren, a merlin and a crested coot. A mustached warbler trailed a goose. A cormorant followed a passenger pigeon, which was followed by a stork, a poppinjay, and a swallow.

"One by one, with blinking speed, the birds rose from the Garden and entered the line of flight that was like a wivvery arrow pointing from the Garden to the pentacle. It was a long, long line. The red-necked grebe, the oriole, the robin red-breast, the pouter pigeon and the cockatoo flew after each other, tail to beak. The quail, flying higher than its wont, pursued the Lapland bunting; the swift, the bluewinged teal, the bouncing petrel and the pygmy owl ruffled the air in their flight.

"One by one, first in their hundreds, then in their thousands, and at last in their swollen millions, the birds took to the sky until the Garden was hidden by the cloud of their numbers.

"Long before the first chickadee was near enough to be seen, the odors of the birds reached us. Songbird or flesheater, marsh bird or mountain fowl, prairie or sea bird, they came on, their wings churning the air, sending the smell of their hot blood before them.

"They came on. Nightingales, warblers, creepers, moorhens, widgeons, alligator birds. The sound of their wings set our valley throbbing. Tree larks, willow wrens; the oven bird, the booby; the yellow-tufted fly-catcher and the heron beat the air, warming and polluting it with their swift exhalations. The starlings from the ruined stables joined the line of flight right behind the limpkins. They were followed by dovekie, murrelet and grouse.

"The air vibrated with their coming. What had been a thin line of birds thickened to a mighty whirring arrow whose shaft was five miles broad and hundreds of miles long.

"Baldur stood, a firm, fixed statue of triumph. As the chickadee, the first bird to leave the Garden, neared us, Baldur spoke to the birds. His voice, high pitched now, pierced the air as he cried, *Anth*, then *Ink*, and finally *Akh hthmmm*. When he moved his right arm imperiously, the chickadee, which had been flying due east, turned and made an arc that brought it into the pentacle midway between its two southern points. The current of birds behind it also turned, and for the rest of the time that the birds flew, the line of their flight took on the shape of a question mark, or of a shepherd's crook, as the birds followed the chickadee's lead.

"On they came and on, their wings making a low rubbing sound, like a dry wind blowing through a barn. As they came closer, that sound turned into an ominous whining, as if sirens were sounding under clouds of dust. Inside the pentacle, the lead birds following the chickadee slowed, preparing to make their gift of feathers on my mother's grave.

"I held my breath and watched the chickadee fall head down, like a stone. Behind it, the cuckoo, the royal eagle, the honey buzzard, the golden plover, the lapwing, the phalarope, the hoopoe, the kingfisher and the nightjar each plummeted in turn.

"Down they dropped. Not twenty feet above the grave, the chickadee came to life and furiously fluttered its wings. I waited for its tiny head to bend to its breast; I waited for it to pluck the single feather it would contribute to my mother's monument.

"It never bent its neck. It never plucked a feather. Instead, the chickadee quivered and gave an impudent flirt with its tail feathers, the unmistakable gesture a bird makes when purging itself in flight. There was a brief white jet, and the chickadee was off, flying at a lower altitude out of the pentacle.

"Down dropped the cuckoo, the eagle, the buzzard. Each bird pulled up, quivered, flirted its tail-feathers, spurted and then flew on. The plover, the merlin, the lark, the dove, the swan, the horned owl, the sparrow and the starling. The crested coot, the goose, the mustached warbler, the swallow. The air no longer hummed; it roared. The mountain that was to have been of feathers, and was not of feathers, grew.

"For a long time I stood unable to watch anything but the birds. At last I looked toward Baldur. He was still poised in the attitude of triumph, but now his face had turned ashen gray. His eyes, which a short while ago had burned in their sockets, seemed to have turned to cinders. From his bitten lower lip, a trickle of blood flowed. His left cheek twitched, as if it were rejecting a fly.

"The birds came on and Baldur stood where he was. The air was thick and hot and fetid. Still Baldur did not move. Finally, I left my corner of the pentacle, and, keeping well away from its shimmering base, I went around to him.

"Putting both my hands to his face, I forced him to look into my eyes. My mutilated lips tried to form words. 'Ohhhhh,' I said. I shook him by the shoulders and tried again to utter words, but I could not sound them. The gash in my upper lip had never been so wide. Finally, I managed 'Sssssssay . . . ssssssomething . . .'

"Baldur was silent. It was still a warm spring morning. Overhead, the birds formed their pulsating question mark in the sky. My mother's monument grew higher with every passing moment. When I closed my eyes I still had to deal with the unrelenting splatter that sounded in my ears.

"All that day, and all that night the mountain grew, until the following dawn when the last turkey buzzard lifted its tail feathers and trailed the last cowbird back to the Garden from which the birds had been called."

XV

"WHAT a terrible story," I said.

"Yes. It was an atrocious mountain," Fritz said.

"I was thinking of your mother," I replied. "How shameful. How repulsive. And you burned her aviaries?"

"Yes, but that was before the monument. It was a simple arson with a humanitarian purpose. After my mother's death, there was no one to look after her birds. Better, Baldur argued, a quick death in the flames than lingering starvation. Besides, several thousand of the birds got away."

"You had no animus against your brother? You followed his lead willingly?" I asked.

"Do you mean did I hate my brother? Often, often. But yes, I followed his lead. It was a way to deserve his attention."

"Even when he entombed your mother so horribly?"

"That was not his fault. Something went wrong with his spells."

"You believe that? You who have read her daybook and who told me the story of how he turned her into a turkey buzzard."

"That was in a dream. I said it was."

"You also said that you weren't sure. You said, too, that Baldur never forgave your mother for that exchange of hearts. Can't you see? He hated her. He planned that abominable mountain. There was no failure of his spells. Don't you see that?"

"Oh, no. He was shaken by it. Shaken."

"By the magnitude of what he had wrought. Not by the event itself."

"What do you know about it?" the harelip grumbled. "If you have no brother of your own, it's easy enough to sit in judgment on my story. A brother is flesh of your flesh, but he is also to some degree your enemy. He steals your mother's milk; your father's smile; the warm place by the fire. Get yourself a brother first and then we'll see if you can bring yourself to judge Baldur."

That, I thought, was very clever, very provocative, but I did not rise to the bait and say, "I have a brother. I know only too well what you mean." Fat though I am, I could be as sly as he. I kept still, but that did not keep me from my memories as I sat on that grimy bed within whose interior who knows what vermin stirred. Putting an attentive look on my face, I let Fritz, the harelip, talk while I let my mind go back to the day when *my* mother died.

XVI

IT was the same day on which I killed the ant in the clearing beneath the catalpa tree. I'm not sure just why the Persian brought his entourage to our castle. He was a discerning fellow. Surely he knew that Hans's threat, "You have your warning, old man," was not spoken lightly. Yet there he was at dusk, the rootless mountebank, risking the anger of a prince by setting up his booth in the outer courtyard of our castle. The ape had just begun banging his tiny cymbals when my mother, who was watching from a tower room, sent a servant to invite the old man and his follower in.

How well I remember his light step as he walked through our gloomy corridors. He had bathed and changed his rags for others that were clean and white. His hair and beard were oiled and combed. The slap of his sandals on our marble floors seemed tuneful and gay. The servants who pointed him toward our great banquet hall, receiving his smile of thanks, smiled themselves for minutes after he had passed.

When he and the saffron vendor reached the hall, the courtiers were already in their seats. My mother, seeing the tall old man in white and the young woman beside him all in saffron, rose from her dais at the curve of the U-shaped table and beckoned them to take the places beside her where Hans and I usually sat. At this mark of favor to itinerant strangers, the courtiers gasped. White-lipped, my handsome brother, Hans, took his place without a word while I, fat Klaus, who had despaired of ever seeing the Persian again, glowed.

My mother commanded wine to be poured, then the first meats were brought in and the low lyre music that was always played at dinner in our hall resumed. At the sound of the first chord, the Persian's ape, who was perched on the back of the old man's chair, leaped onto the white tablecloth and pranced amid the plates and goblets. My mother looked on like one transfixed, while the ape, in a sad imitation of a dancer, lurched and leaped.

It was not a lovely creature. Gray and mangy, it seemed profoundly weary. Its eyes were so large, so luminous and dark that it was easy to imagine that there was a look of wisdom hidden in them, wisdom based on a knowledge of pain. Clumsy though the creature's movements were and utterly out of time with the music, I noticed that the animal never disturbed a plate, a goblet or a piece of silverware.

Hans called to the Persian, "Old man, get that beast off my mother's table."

"Here, I'll take him," the saffron grinder said and leaned forward to catch at the ape, but my mother—my sickly, lethargic mother—as if electrified, was there before her. In a most unqueenly gesture, she snatched at the ape and caught it. Holding it to her breast, she said, "Hush, Hans, hush. Oh," and now she rocked the ape in her arms, "Oh, the poor little thing."

The ape pressed its face against her breast, twitched its

wiry arms around her neck, looked up at her with its disappointed eyes, and heaved a voluptuous sigh.

Then began a strange spectacle as the queen, with her two grown sons looking on, rocked the creature as if she had all her life been waiting for a chance to nurse an ape. "Hush, thee, hush thee, little orphan," she crooned, and "Oh, the poor binten."

The creature scratched at a bare patch in its fur, then, its head turning from left to right, it swiveled its gaze around the assembled company after which, with a shameless wave of its hand, it dismissed us all and fell asleep.

"Mother!" It was Hans at his most commanding, "Give the old man his ape." The saffron vendor, too, was on her feet. When the two women met at the edge of the dais, they exchanged a long look of hostility.

The old Persian rose and would have gone to the dais but my mother said, "Stay, good sir." To the saffron grinder, she said, "You, go back to your seat." Then, more gently, she added, "I will not harm the dear creature." The young woman looked from the queen to the Persian. At his nod, she returned reluctantly to her place.

My mother, having made her conciliatory gesture, went back to her throne. As she sat down, she bent and brushed the sleeping animal's face with her cheek. Her eyes still on it, she said, "Persian, my servants tell me that, in addition to being a soothsayer, you are a teller of tales. Tell us one to drive the tedium from our banquet hall."

The Persian bowed. Hans gnawed at his lower lip. His dagger was on the table now, as if he meant to use it to cut his meat.

"Your majesty," the Persian said, "is as kind as she is beautiful." The look of undisguised admiration he turned on her set the roomful of courtiers to buzzing. Hans speared a piece of roast meat with his dagger and proceeded to cut it nervously into squares. "I would, however, with your majesty's permission, like to tell not one tale, but two."

"Why two?" my mother inquired.

"For two reasons: The first is that the number one is the symbol for perfection and I know no perfect tales. The second is that two is the symbol for ambiguity and all tales are ambiguous. Hence, I tell two tales so my listeners can choose the ambiguities that speak to them."

"Come, Persian," said my mother, with a flirtatious toss of her head, "is there no thread that binds the two?"

"Yes, your majesty. Dreams. I tell only tales in which there are dreams."

Now, why my mother blushed at such an innocent remark, I do not know. I only know that she did and that Hans, seeing the scarlet in her cheeks, muttered, "I'll kill him."

"Look at her," I said. "Have you ever seen her so happy?"

He growled, "That's not happiness. She's in heat."

My mother, even before her illness, had never been robust. Her marriage to my father had so wasted her that within a year after the wedding one could see her skull and cheekbones under her nearly transparent skin. Though her dark eyes had grown enormous, they seemed to cower in her cavernous eye sockets.

Born in a tropical kingdom, she had spent her youth, even in that climate, trying to warm her blood, either by crawling deeper under feather beds or by poking up the fires laid for her in various rooms. By day, she carried tin buckets filled with smoldering sawdust at which she tried, futilely, to warm her fingertips. At night, the servants put heated bricks between the sheets of her bed. At any time, muffs, cloaks, scarves, gloves and furs were her preoccupation.

My father, to whom she was delivered after a long sea voyage, was the king of an ice-bound kingdom. Though he found her to be as beautiful as the marriage brokers had promised, he did not take kindly to her shivering, regarding it as a personal affront. It made no difference to him that she had shivered before he knew her. He was determined, in their marriage bed, to make her glow with his body heat. When he accused her, she said through chattering teeth, "My Lord, forgive me, I'm cold." He took her words not as a statement of fact but as a challenge to his technique and went at her more fiercely. He had great confidence in his fingertips and in certain positions and accommodations he had perfected. When my mother continued to shiver, he concluded that she was sensually deformed and let her sleep alone, but that was not until after he had begotten first me, fat Klaus, and then my handsome brother Hans. My mother loved us, but she was distracted by the cold. She would have done anything for us, but we had pity on her and never asked for much. She floated through the castle like a wraith and kept out of my father's way. Occasionally, overcome by a sense of responsibility, she embroidered handkerchiefs for us. What could we do but accept? They were silk handkerchiefs, carefully hemmed. The stitching was so accurate one would never have guessed that the hand that held the needle had been rigid with cold.

Sometimes her long fingers stroked us, or she sang us lullabies in a language we did not understand. Through the years, the darkness in her eyes deepened. She was often very sad and held us to her in a light embrace that left us with the memory of her pale lemon soap and the soft pressure of her unbound breasts.

Four years before the night on which the Persian came to the castle, her physicians determined that she was dying. From that time on, there was never a day that did not have hovering over it an imminent sense of farewell. Yet, now, as the Persian settled into his tale-telling, there she sat, with an effulgent smile on her face, the scabrous ape in the crook of her arm, looking for all the world like a parody of a madonna. Flushed, one would have said, with health, her skin suffused with the sort of glow that comes from happiness.

The Persian, like the practiced speaker that he was, seemed to be looking directly at her while he talked even as he addressed the courtiers and their ladies sitting at the U-shaped table.

XVII

"NOT so very long ago," the Persian was saying, "the animals could talk as well as we can. The quickest-witted of them all was Reynard, the fox, who, in addition to his glib tongue, was notorious for his thievery, his gluttony and the tricks by means of which he crammed his gullet. For the sake of his stomach, he kept no oath, was faithful to no friendship and was utterly and always a stranger to the truth. Though he was known far and wide as a trickster and betrayer, he had such a persuasive, lying tongue that many a forest creature succumbed to his wiles.

"Now it happened in those days that there was a prosperous farmer who lived in a large house at the edge of the wood. The house was built of oak and shingled with cedar. Its rooms were wide and spacious, its pantry and larder well stocked with hams and bacon, with flour and lard and butter and cheese and with the excellent spices with which such foods are made bright to the tongue: coriander, ginger, sage, saffron and thyme.

"In his pens, there were sheep and goats. In his barns there were red cows and brown, red bulls and black; in his stables there were draft horses and ponies and high-mettled steeds.

"But the farmer's pride and joy was his barnyard in which geese and ducks paddled in ponds; pea-hens and peacocks strutted; slack-wattled turkeys strolled. He had a score of hens, red, black, and white, that clucked and pecked, all of them lorded over by the rooster Chanticleer who, when the humor was on him, flew down from whatever high perch he was on to refresh himself and one of his hens. He was a lord at all degrees, with a bright red comb and black and gold throat feathers that shimmered in the sun and blue-black tail-feathers that arched behind him like a valiant pennon. When, at dawn, he threw back his head, fluffed out his tail and crowed the morning in, all who heard him believed that they could hear in it a local echo of the music of the spheres.

"Now, it was this proud Chanticleer's bones that the fox, Reynard of Evil Counsel, was determined to gnaw. Often had he peered through the spiky hedge that surrounded the barnyard and admired Chanticleer's proud walk and his frequent flights to refresh himself with one of his hens. 'That cock,' Reynard mused, 'should prove most succulent and his vigor, when I make a meal of him, will pass from his flesh to mine.'

"Sly though Reynard was, he could not get past the spiky thorn bush hedges with which the farmer had enclosed the barnyard. Four separate times, Reynard tried to squeeze past them but their long, sharp thorns inflicted cruel gashes on his nose and sides. Six times, he had tried to overleap the brake, but he had only bruised muscles to show for his pains.

"And so Reynard bided his time–and dreamed of the day that Chanticleer would be his.

"Meanwhile, Chanticleer, too, was having dreams. But his dreams were vague and ominous. It seemed to him that while he slept, some *thing* with a red aspect appeared to him. Red in its upper parts, and pale red at its belly; and the thing had bright yellow eyes, and ears that pricked up; and a red plume behind that swayed with a martial air. What terrified the dreaming Chanticleer was that the creature was moving through the barnyard with a malign intent.

"Then Chanticleer, in his dream, knew what the Thing was searching for. 'Me,' Chanticleer groaned. 'The thing wants me.' Just then, the Thing in the dream turned and opened wide its huge maw and Chanticleer found himself staring up at a glistening red glottis. He uttered a pathetic cry, like air escaping from a bladder, 'Cock-a-doodle-deeeeeeee,' then he shuddered and woke up.

"Exhausted, his eyes bleary, his head aching, he sought out Pertelote, the little red hen, the fairest of his consorts, to whom he confided what he had dreamed. 'A shape, huge and ghastly. With eyes and teeth. Red and pale red. With a tail. A gargoyle in the barnyard.'

"'Ah, Chanticleer. Is this how the hero whom I married behaves? You, who crow the sun up every morning. Fie upon it. And on you. To let a dream make a coward of you. Ask me, 'What is a dream?' and I reply "It is the merest product of indigestion.' Shame on you. You swallow a tough worm or a bad seed and you are all transformed and stand here pale and trembling. A sulfur purge is what you need.'

"'No,' insisted Chanticleer. "'I saw what I saw. There is some lowering evil near the barnyard. Let you, Pertelote, and all my other hens, take care. Ware the russet monster.'

"And 'Ware the russet monster,' cried all the other hens. The cry was honked by the geese and quacked by the ducks and whistled by the swans and gobbled by the turkeys. 'Ware the russet monster.'

"The russet monster on the other side of the thorn brake heard their cries and was inspired by the Evil One to crawl on his belly along the base of the hedge searching once more for some tear or gap. This time, lo and behold he found one. A hole through which a badger or a polecat had crawled only yesterday.

"Sharp-eyed Madame Pinte, one of Chanticleer's under-wives, who was just then pecking up gravel for her crop, caught sight of the fox and sounded the alarm. 'He's here. The russet monster's here,' she cried and Chanticleer, his wives and every other fowl in the barnyard flew or scurried or swam for shelter: the hens and turkeys to perches in the barn; the ducks and hens into the middle of the pond; the pea-fowl to the railing of the well while Chanticleer, more foolhardy than the rest, flapped his way to the nearby tip of the manure pile.

"With a courtly wave of his tail, the fox said, 'Ah, Lord Chanticleer, good health to you. I trust you have not flown away from any fear of me. Let me introduce myself, Reynard, the fox.'

"'Keep your distance, Reynard,' said Chanticleer. 'I know who you are. You are the russet monster of my dream.'

"'Russet, yes. Monster, no,' said Reynard. 'What I am is a lover of fine music who has admired your family's talents for three generations. I heard your grandfather crow up the sun on the day after the Great Eclipse. Many a time have I heard your father, of blessed memory. Where was the cock who could sing like him? Who can forget him, standing on tiptoes, his eyes closed, summoning up the morning in a voice so loud it could be heard five leagues away? What clarity of tone; what sweetness, what suavity.'

"Flattery, the great elixir of deceit, has led to the downfall of kings and potentates. Is it any wonder, then, that the flattered Chanticleer, preening on his dunghill, replied, 'Really? You want to hear me sing?'

" 'Yes. But loudly, my lord. Like your father, with his eyes closed and his head thrown back.'

"Chanticleer took a deep breath. Then a shadow crossed his face as he remembered his dream. 'No, Reynard. I don't trust you. Back off. There, farther back.'

"The fox willingly drew back. Then Chanticleer closed his eyes, stretched up on his tiptoes, spread his wings and began what was meant to be his longest, loudest, most sonorous crow.

"As Reynard knew it would, that trance of self-adulation lasted a very long time. *Cock-a-doodle-dooooooooooooo*, called Chanticleer. The fox leaped and was on Chanticleer before he could achieve his final *doooo*.

"In another instant, the fox, with the hapless Chanticleer in his jaws, was through the hole in the thorn brake and running as fast as could be toward his den on the other side of the stream that bordered the farmer's wheat field.

"The hens, the ducks, the geese, the turkeys and the pea-fowl, witnesses to the abduction of Chanticleer, set up such a great quacking and clucking and honking and trumpeting and gobbling that it brought the farmer's wife out of the house. When she saw the fox sprinting through the wheat field with Chanticleer slung over his shoulder, she added her voice to the din, 'Help, Dikkon, Nikkon, Tyrnon and Twyll. The fox has stolen Chanticleer.'

"Dikkon, Nikkon, Tyrnon and Twyll, who were in the green wheat field digging up weeds with their hoes, seeing the fox's russet tail and catching a glimpse of Chanticleer's blue-black tail-feathers, waved their hoes and set off in pursuit, whistling up their dogs as they ran.

"The dogs, sixteen in number, streaked through the green wheat field after the fox. The baying of the hounds excited other farm hands and dogs to join the chase and soon there were three-score men and animals pursuing Reynard. There were cries of 'Harrow' and 'Tallyho.' 'Thief,' 'scoundrel,' 'murderer' and other names too foul to be repeated were called after him. The beleaguered Reynard's exultation faded and he settled to the grim task of escape.

"Chanticleer, though initially half dead with fright, had had a little time to bethink himself. In a strangled voice (his head, after all, was in the fox's mouth), he called, 'Reynard! Reynard! Where is your self respect? Do you hear the names they are calling you? Will you let such insults go unanswered?'

"His pride touched to the quick, Reynard, master beguiler of others, was now himself beguiled. Panting and weary, he turned nevertheless to face his pursuers and called, 'Scurvy louts. I defy you.'

"The first word was no sooner out of the fox's mouth when Chanticleer tore himself loose and, with a mighty flapping of wings, flew into the boughs of a nearby apple tree. 'Well,' he called down to the baffled fox, 'what do you say, sly fellow? What is the moral of our story?'

"The dejected fox looked hungrily up at the triumphant Chanticleer. 'There's a time to speak, and a time to keep still, and it's a poor fool who cannot tell what time it is.'

"Full of wrath and rancor, he would have said more, but by then the hounds and the men were nearly on him so, choosing the better part of valor:

> He turned tail and away he ran,
> And my tale ends where it began.

XVIII

THERE was a round of such warm applause from the courtiers that it roused the ape sleeping in my mother's arms. The beast lifted its head, rolled its eyes, looked vaguely around the banquet hall and made a sound like a human infant weeping. My mother caressed its forehead and whispered, "Hush, little orphan. Hush." The ape looked up into her eyes, wriggled closer against her and went back to sleep.

"Your tale, Persian," my mother said, "has a rough charm. You move your narrative along at a brisk pace and the moral of the tale, as the fox announces it, is simple and apt. But, taken all in all, it seems a tale fitter to be told to toilers pausing in a marketplace than to an assembly in a royal banquet hall. Come, sir soothsayer, let me keep you to your word. You have cautioned us not to expect perfection, but where is the ambiguity you promised?" All of this my mother said in a manner so openly flirtatious that it set the courtiers buzzing. The saffron vendor tore morsels from a flap of bread and rolled them into tiny balls. Hans, whose teeth I could hear grinding, drove the tip of his dagger into the table top, where it stood, quivering.

The Persian smiled, "Your majesty is pleased to seem perplexed though I think you are not so. Before I tell my second story, you may want to consider the mysteries that lie hidden in this one. For instance, what does the tale intend? To display the fox's wisdom, or Chanticleer's? Chanticleer's foolishness or the fox's? As for ambiguity, what shall we say of Pertelote, the red hen? Are not her theory of dreams and her scoffing at Chanticleer to some degree mischievous? May they not bespeak a domestic situation in which the cock is more nearly a victim than a tyrant? Why, what could be more ambiguous than the possibility that Madame Pertelote is the russet monster of Chanticleer's dream?"

"And how would you answer those questions?"

"Your highness surely knows that it is in the nature of a tale-teller to tell, but there is nothing in his profession that requires him to know."

"Ah, sir," laughed my mother, "that was prettily evaded. Well, well. No one will ever accuse you of being at a loss for words. But how like a man to have us believe that instead of 'Ware the russet fox' the cry of alarm in the barnyard should have been 'Ware the little red hen.' Never mind. Tell your second tale, but this time keep us out of the barnyard. Give us a story of lords and ladies . . . "

"A dream tale," the Persian insisted affably, "and a tale of love."

"Oh yes," my mother whispered as she rocked the ape in her arms. "A dream tale . . . and a tale of love."

XIX

"IN a faraway kingdom," the Persian began, "there was a king who was as powerful as he was wise. He had subdued the kingdoms on his borders and had established his peace over a vast domain. With no further conquests demanded of him, he disbanded his armies and divided his time daily between the dispensation of justice and the pursuit of his forest deer.

"Once, on a hot July day, he and a dozen of his courtiers chased a twelve-pronged stag for the greater part of the morning only to have it elude them. Exhausted, the king called a halt in a barley field. There, his courtiers spread out a saddle blanket and the king lay down three paces from his tethered horse. What with the fatigue of the hunt and the warmth of the sun, it was not long before he fell asleep.

"In his fitful sleep, he dreamed, and in his dream he knew himself to be in a distant land of dense forests, blue lakes, and snow-covered mountains that reached the sky. In that land, he, the king, was on foot, walking on a well-laid-out road on the slope of a great mountain. Before him, a mile or so away, there loomed a turreted castle on whose several towers pennons fluttered in the breeze.

"The king walked toward the castle, impressed at once by the beauty of the countryside and by the sense of apprehension that it roused in him. Still, as he was a king unused to fear, he strode on boldly until he came to the portcullis of the castle. There he shouted, 'Ho, sentries at the gate. Here am I. Let me in.'

"There were two sentries, one clad in red, the other in black, on either side of the watchtower. The one in red cried down, 'Who calls?' and the one in black called, 'Who asks to be let in?'

"I, a king."

"The red-clad sentry said, 'Here, none but wise kings are admitted. Are you wise?'

" 'I know what I know.' "

" 'And what do you know?' asked the sentry in black.

" 'I know that I am a king inside a dream.'

" 'If you know that,' said the red-clad sentry, 'then you are wise, enter.' With that, they raised the portcullis and the king walked in.

"He went from one spacious hall to another. From white marble to black, from black to green and from green to onyx. Everywhere he walked there were high windows of cut glass set in lead depicting scenes of love. In the glow of sunlight surging through the colored glass, the king saw gods disporting themselves with mortal women, old men peering through shrubbery at nubile girls bathing in pools. He saw heroes in flight from the rage of cuckolded husbands and he saw kings entwined in the arms of barmaids, and queens disporting themselves in the beds of stable boys.

"As he walked, the king's sense of apprehension grew. Then, at the top of a staircase, he turned to the right and entered a cheerful but dimly lit chamber whose walls were of polished apple wood. In the center of this room, there were two young men sitting at an ivory table playing chess while an old man sat nearby at a bench carving chessmen out of gold.

"So much the king saw in his dream, but neither the chess players nor the old man caused the king any apprehension. And yet, he knew that where he was was dangerous.

"Then in a corner of the room beside a window that looked out over a garden, he saw the princess. Her gown of silk was green and gold, her unbound golden hair spilled down over her shoulders and reached to her waist. Her forehead was broad, her eyes hazel. Her skin was white as milk and her lips were delicate and full. In her right hand, she held a silver pencil with which she had just written something on a tablet that lay in her lap.

"Though he could not rid himself of the feeling that something ominous was about to happen, the king moved toward her until he was close enough to read her words. They were, 'I love . . . '

"The maiden looked up. Seeing the king, she smiled, put her book and pencil aside and rose to greet him. He enfolded her in his arms and pressed his lips to hers. There was the scent of plum blossoms blowing in from the garden, and the maiden's sweet breath in his nostrils. The king grew giddy, but just then the sun's heat in the barley field where he slept so oppressed his breathing that he woke.

"Then began a sorry time in the young king's life. Unable to sleep, unable to eat, he paced his corridors. He sat for hours in his study which, now, he kept dark except for a single candle by whose light he studied the pattern of his rug or the shadows playing on his wall. When he was not sighing, he wrote in a day book verses over which he shed tears: rondels, rondeaus, triolets and villanelles.

"The months passed and the king did not take his place in the council chamber nor did he sit on his throne dispensing justice to his subjects as he had been wont to do.

"Little by little, the evils that wait to beset a kingdom crept out of the hiding places into which, in former days, he had driven them. Once more, the rich oppressed the poor; the powerful abused the weak. Greed and luxury replaced temperance and propriety as the normal habits of the court.

"This sorry state of affairs continued until one day an honest courtier risked his life and said to the king, 'Your majesty, you are ill-spoken of in the kingdom.'

"'Why is that?' asked the king.

"'Because it is many months since you have sat in council; and many months since you gave over dispensing justice. Your people murmur because once again the rich oppress the poor, the powerful torment the weak, and evil, unhindered, struts about the land.'

"'Ah,' sighed the king. 'Would it were not so, but I can do nothing so long as my heart is sad.' He hid his face in his hands.

"The loyal courtier persisted, 'What makes you sad, my lord?'

"The king then told him of his dream in the barley field. Of the castle, the towers with the pennons flying, the warders in red and black, the great halls and the wood-paneled room in which the young chess players sat while an old man carved chessmen out of gold. Finally, he told him about the maiden, her tablet, her pencil and her fragrant kiss.

"The courtier said, 'Your Highness, the poor and powerless can do no more than wake from their dreams, but kings may shape them. If you want the princess, find her.'

" 'The king thanked the honest courtier and left him in charge of his kingdom. Then he mounted his horse and traveled the wide world over. Ten years passed until one day he came to a fair land of dense forests and blue lakes and of mountains that reached the sky. His horse trotted on a well laid out road on the slope of a mountain. There, as in his dream, he saw, a mile or so before him, a castle from whose turrets there were pennons flying.

"When he came to the castle, there again, on either side of the watchtower over the portcullis, were the two warders, one clad in black, the other in red. The king called up to them, 'Ho, warders at the gate, let me in.'

"The warder in black called down, 'Who asks to be let in?'

" 'I, a king.'

"The warder in red cried, 'Here, none but wise kings are admitted. Are you wise?'

" 'I know what I know,' said the king.

" 'And what do you know?' asked the warder in black.

" 'I know that I am a king awake.'

" 'If you know that,' said the warder in red, 'then you are wise. Enter.' And the king strode in.

"The king passed through the great halls he had seen in his dream and saw as before the light streaming through the high windows of colored glass in which scenes of love were depicted. At last he came to the room paneled in apple wood and there were the two young men playing chess at an ivory table while an old man sat at a bench nearby carving chessmen out of gold.

"The king looked around the room and marveled that all was as it had been in his dream. However, when he saw the princess in her green-and-gold gown and the tablet in her lap with the words 'I love . . . ' written on it, he was assailed again by a sense of apprehension. Still, he stepped forward, and the princess, seeing him, put down her tablet and pencil and rose to greet him.

"The next instant she was in his arms, but as he bent to kiss her golden hair, her white skin, her hazel eyes dissolved. His lips sought hers but could not find them. Her hand at his face was dry, bony and hard. He heard her say, 'Kiss me, Majesty, and I am yours.' He, uncertain and afraid, whispered, 'Yes. Perhaps.' He bent his head but from the garden below her window there came the sound of bridle bells and the clanking of armor and a gust of wind that stank of horse piss.

"He would have swooned except his head struck a hummock and he woke to find himself sprawled on a saddle blanket in the barley field surrounded by a dozen of his courtiers. He was sweating from the sun's heat. His head ached, his eyelids were gummy, his tongue was rough and dry. Not three paces away, his bay stallion, its hind legs spread, was still sending a great steaming yellow stream into the dust.

"And this tale of love is called 'A King Dreams of Love in a Barley Field,' and now I make an end to it."

XX

FROM the restrained applause that followed the Persian's tale it was clear that the courtiers liked his earlier barnyard story better than this one of a sleeping king.

Actually, I found his tale exhilarating. Especially the replies the king made to the two warders on the turrets: "I know I am a king inside a dream" and "I know that I am a king awake." My mother, on the other hand, looked doubtful. She sat for a while in a brown study, then she said, "Your tale of love, soothsayer, is unlike any we are used to hearing from the minstrels who pass through our realm. They tell of lovers' hopes deferred or disappointed by cruel husbands, of wicked giants, or fire-breathing dragons. But always, the heroes persevere and rescue the beautiful maidens from perils unspeakable. Then the lovers sink into each other's arms as into a well of bliss. But in your tale . . . your tale . . . "

Here, she crimsoned. Hans poked the hilt of his dagger into my thigh and said under his breath, "That man is his own death warrant."

The Persian nodded, "Your Majesty is right," he said. "In my story, there are no battles to the death, no miraculous escapes from dismal dungeons. But surely you will agree that what my tale lacks in the way of adventure, it makes up for in ambiguity."

"Oh yes," my mother said hurriedly. "Ambiguity. Your favorite word." Then, beaming prettily, like a schoolgirl attempting to disarm a watchful schoolmaster, she said, "Yes. The tale does pose questions that cry out for answers." And now her manner of speech candidly mimicked the Persian's. "What shall we make of the princess who seems ready to kiss all passing strangers? And whose name is she about to write on her tablet? And what is the meaning of that horrible detail, her dissolving face? Well, soothsayer, what do you reply?"

"Ah, madam, as I have said, the tale-teller's task is to tell. It is no part of his duty to know."

Hans could contain himself no longer. He pounded on the table with the hilt of his dagger. "Mother! This mountebank goes about selling confusion. I've had more than enough of his lying tricks. Let me cut his throat and be done with him."

My mother rose and, passing the sleeping ape over to its master, stood for a moment as poised as a caryatid. In the torch light, the green silk of her gown shimmered. She looked young and regal and powerful. "Hans," she said, "this scholar is our guest and as such is protected by the laws of hospitality."

"He makes trouble as the sparks fly upward. If you cannot manage him, let me have him. Can't you see he is insulting you?"

"He's doing no such thing. He is a man of the world. Widely experienced. We can learn much from him."

"I'll cut his throat," said Hans.

"Careful, Hans. Careful," she said. The saffron vendor had risen to her feet and was standing in a half-crouch looking watchfully first at my brother, then at the Persian and finally at my mother. The Persian, calmly stroking his sleeping ape, looked around the room as if prudently searching for an exit. Oblivious of the staring courtiers, my mother turned to the Persian and, as if she were sharing a problem with a husband with whom she had lived for many years, asked, "What makes the boy so irritable, I wonder?"

The soothsayer continued to pat his ape's head as he said, "Your majesty, I chanced to offend your son today in the marketplace. At his insistence, and against my will, I turned my cockatoo loose to find him a token or a sign. I warned the prince that I know nothing; that my bird is only a bird, though sometimes we stumble on clues from on high. Your son did not like the omen my bird found for him."

"No," Hans said. "Because there was chicanery, trickery, deceit. That man's very presence here in our hall is a stain on our honor."

"Your Highness," the Persian bowed and made a gesture with his arm that acknowledged the presence of the courtiers, "I understand the prince's irritation. Sometimes my bird finds a token that can frighten its buyer. Fear begets anger and . . . "

Hans was on his feet, the cords in his neck rigid. "Damn you and your lying cards. I fear nothing. Not you, not your bird, not your tokens. Nothing."

The saffron vendor, who had left her seat and was inching her way toward the Persian, now plucked at his sleeve. "Come away," she whispered. "This is a bad household. No good can come of our being here. Come away."

"Hush," he replied, giving her a hasty caress.

"No," she cried. "No. I know why you won't go. It's because of her."

"What is it?" my mother cried. "What's happening? What does she want?"

"Ah mother, mother, mother," Hans panted, "you ought to be ashamed of yourself, at your age."

"Come away," the saffron vendor begged, still plucking at the Persian's sleeve. "Can't you see? Just look at her, the woman's cold."

My heart sank. From what recess of female wisdom had she plucked that word 'cold'?

My mother, her cheeks aflame, whirled. Her nostrils flaring, her lower lip thrust out, she all but screamed, "Get that baggage out of here!" Three courtiers were instantly on their feet and wrestling with the young woman.

"Come away," the saffron vendor cried from out of the melée. "She isn't worth it."

Shaken, the Persian turned from her to my mother. "Your Majesty . . . ," he began, then he turned to the saffron vendor. "Go now. It's only for a little while. Nothing has changed. Go, child."

"I'm not a child," she wailed as the courtiers dragged her away. From the outer hallway, and over the sound of her sliding heels, there came her laughter and then her hollow cry, "Cold. The woman's an icicle."

In the banquet hall, we were all silent, as if we had been suddenly turned into figures in a tapestry. I sat, remembering my encounter with the saffron-scented woman in the glade beneath the catalpa tree. For all of its confused ending, there had been a glaze of sweetness over that event.

Hans brooded beside me. My mother, her face still flushed, resumed her seat on the dais. Turning to the Persian, she said, "Those omens your bird chooses. Are they dangerous?"

"Your Majesty, omens, like tales, can be dark. For those who cannot abide uncertainty, what is hidden or half-revealed can seem dangerous. I cannot blame any man for being afraid . . . "

"Afraid! Afraid!" Hans, his eyes sparkling, was on his feet. "Damn you Persian, turn loose your bird. Here. Now. We'll see who's afraid."

The Persian looked toward my mother. "Your Majesty, I have once already offended your son. I would much prefer . . . "

My mother interrupted, "You would not hurt him, would you?"

"I would not hurt you for the world."

"Why then," she said serenely, "do what Hans asks, since no harm can come of it."

"I did not say . . . "

"You have heard the queen, Persian. Turn loose your bird."

The old man shrugged. Sadly, patiently, he reached behind him for his bird cage and set it on the table. Then, with a decided motion, he plucked the cloth cover from the cage. The cockatoo let out an indignant squawk that woke the ape. With a bark like a child coughing, the scruffy beast leaped from its master's lap to his shoulder, from which, looking like a gnome, it peered around the room.

"Come on," Hans growled, "get this charade over with."

"You are agitated, prince. You are vexed. Perhaps another time would be better."

"Now," said Hans. "This minute. Turn loose your bird for me."

The Persian nodded. "Very well. But first, as you recall, there must be a coin."

Hans flung a silver coin toward the old man, who caught it and, without looking at it, put it into a fold in his rags. That done, he bent to open the door of the cage.

"Observe, your Highness," the Persian began. "Observe, courtiers and ladies." As he spoke, his voice assumed again the pitch and rhythm he had used in the marketplace. "I hold in my hand a packet of cards on which are inscribed tokens and signs. The cards are in random order. Now, as you see, I remove them one by one from the top of the pack and tuck them . . . so . . . into the lattice work of the cage. Here and there. Here and there. Always at random. Entirely without program or plan. A child would be more orderly. An ape or an idiot would achieve more design. And now, observe! I bend. I unlatch the cage door and open it. Now, I step back. One step. Another. You will observe that there is nothing in my hands. That I am now three paces from the cage.

"Watch closely. Jauntily the bird steps from its little home. It looks around . . . " Here, I tried desperately to think of something I might do that would keep the events that were to come from happening. If I could only create a distraction, I might save *someone*: my mother, the Persian, Hans, the saffron vendor, myself. I sat and waited, hoping that the right idea would come to me. Some bright imperative to shout or stand on my head or to make a speech so wise that I could draw everyone's attention to me. But, alas, I have neither a quick mind nor a stout heart. Such ideas as came to me seemed either unworkable or required more courage than I could muster. So I sat there, a great, helpless fat man, thinking regretful thoughts of the spoke I *might* have put in destiny's wheel if I had had the courage. Instead I did what I and cowards always do — I watched.

In that hot room, amid the smells of wine and roasted meat, the newly released bird looked around. It cocked its head and listened, standing daintily on one foot. Then the cockatoo, its bright yellow eyes intent on the cards stuck around the lattice of its cage, hopped toward them. It fluttered its wings and clucked.

The ape, scratching at a flea or at a scab, clung to its master's shoulder. The cockatoo hopped and walked among crusts of bread, over pools of spilled wine and the bones of other birds. Around the cage it moved, as if searching for a particular card. Once, it was distracted by an unshelled almond it found in its way. It stopped and, with a quick motion, had the nut in its beak. There was a tiny snapping sound and bits of shell fell to the table, as the bird swallowed the almond.

The bird hopped, or walked. It fluttered toward the cage and away from it. Then, there was a confused instant after which there was the bird with a bit of pasteboard in its beak. Softly the Persian called, "Now. Give it to the prince."

The bird moved reluctantly in Hans's direction. Several times it veered away only to resume its hopping toward him. When at last it stood before him it made an awkward motion that seemed like a bow and presented the

card in its beak to him. Hans, pale as a sheet, took it and
studied it as the bird clucked and hurried back to its cage,
knocking over whatever wine glasses, silverware and strewn
bits of bread and meat stood in its way.

"Persian!" It was my mother gasping for help. Slumped
in her chair, she looked suddenly waxen, as if all the warmth
with which her body had been suffused since the arrival of
the soothsayer had drained out of her. Her breathing was
shallow, her thin shoulders drooped. "Persian!" Her hands
pressed the arms of her chair as she tried to rally the strength
to stand. "The card . . . Hans . . . Don't let it frighten
him . . . " In an instant, the old man was beside the throne
and had her in his arms. Her head against his breast, she
heaved a great sigh. "He is so young . . . so stern."

"There," the Persian said. "There, there." He reached
for a wine glass and put it to her lips. To please him, she
tried to take a few sips of the wine but could not manage it.

Hans, holding the card the cockatoo had given him in
his left hand and his unsheathed dagger by the blade in his
right was also on his feet. "Mountebank! You dare to touch
the queen? Put her down or die."

My mother's eyes closed then opened. "Hans," she whispered. "Klaus." At the sound of my name, I felt my heart turn
over. Her arm went around the Persian's neck. "Hold me,"
she begged. "Hold me . . . Farewell." The Persian, white-
haired, strong-featured and tall, held her, rocked her.

"Farewell," he said. "Farewell." He looked, for a while,
into her eyes, then he closed them gently.

So that was the end of my mother.

All her life she had been cold; and for the last four years
she had been dying, and now, strangely unlooked for, here

was her death come around at last. "How parsimonious of fate," I thought, "to wait until her final hour to give her a man into whose eyes she could look with love."

Hans was not of my opinion. The sight of my mother dead in the old man's arms enraged him. His lips compressed, his eyes narrowed, then he shouted, "Die, Persian. Die," and threw his dagger.

There was an ugly cry and the ape, which had scrambled back onto the table in the commotion following my mother's seizure, fell forward, the handle of Hans's dagger protruding from its throat.

The Persian, still weeping for my mother, groaned and looked for some place to set her down so he could tend to his ape. Inside its cage, the cockatoo rattled the wires hysterically. The Persian, my mother still in the crook of his right arm, knelt beside the bleeding ape. "Hush," he said, caressing its forehead as he tried to still its cries. "Hush, little darling. Hush."

I stood behind the soothsayer and patted his shoulder, but Hans thrust me aside and spun the old man about. When Hans plucked his dagger from the ape's throat, I thought, "Ah, the old man's time has come." But Hans only wiped the dagger clean and thrust it back into his scabbard. Looking down at my mother, who looked comfortably ensconced in the old man's arm, Hans dropped the card the bird had given him into her lap and said, "See, mother. See what you've done." With that he turned on his heel and strode out of the hall.

When the courtiers took my mother's body from the Persian's arms and carried it to her chamber, Hans's card dropped from her lap to the floor. I picked it up and studied it.

Slowly, the banquet hall emptied until only the weeping old man, the corpse of his ape and I were left. The torches glimmered and the fire in the fireplace died down. Still, there was enough light left in the hall so I could read my brother's card.

Finally, I let it drop. It was, as my mother and the Persian must have known, blank.

I stood silently beside the bowed Persian. I was a huge, fat man who had failed to outwit disaster. On the tile roof over the hall, there sounded the patter of our long-awaited rain.

XXI

THE harelip was saying, "You, sir. You have the *look* of a man who is listening. Are you listening?"

"Of course I am." What did he expect me to say? While I was caressing my memories, he had been grinding away, sending his words across the space between us and, with one ear, I took them all in. It is not a difficult trick, to know what has been said without really paying attention. The harelip was so little attentive to my reply that he did not hear its note of insincerity and plunged on. Telling, telling.

I, meanwhile, sank back into my own memories of Hans and the saffron vendor after my mother died. For a week after her funeral, Hans paced the corridors, his heels clicking on the stone as he meditated revenge against the Persian.

Hans! Whose quaint conceit is that he was not born. What was it he had written on the harelip's postcard?

" . . . I am nobody's brother. I was not born. From the beginning, I had more memories than if I had lived a thousand years . . . "

What childish fancies. What was all that hard contempt for the world except another form of self-loathing. I know that he was born because I was there when the nurse brought him in, a piece of inert, shrunken flesh she was about to dispose of.

In the dramatic hubbub of my mother's childbed scene, I, the fat two-year-old had been overlooked. Frightened at being shunted from one room in the palace to another, I had slipped into the birth chamber and found a corner in which to cower. I heard my mother's groans and stopped my ears against her shrieks. When someone in the room cried out, "Oh my god, the baby is . . . " I scuttled over to the trash bin where I hoped to hide but I was followed by the midwife who brought my limp, cold brother over to the bucket reserved for such accidents. She had already lifted the lid and was about to drop him in when I cried, "Wait!" The midwife was so impressed with the authority that issued from the lips of a two-year-old that she obeyed.

"Show me," I commanded.

She held Hans's wrinkled, bloodstained body out. His eyes were closed, his tiny legs turned in like withered branches. My mother, in another corner of the room, whimpered, too exhausted to know what had happened. My father was in another part of the castle acquiring from a young gypsy woman the sporting illness that would kill him later in the year.

"Hold him still," I said and the midwife, mesmerized, obeyed. I stared down at the shriveled body. His head was large, his shoulders were narrow and sloping, his chest was sunken and there was no breath in him. No breath at all. At first, I prodded his temple, then his stomach, with the fat forefinger of my right hand. Nothing happened. Then with the wisdom that comes from memories of lifetimes not our own, I knew what to do. I tensed my middle finger against my thumb and allowed pressure to build inside the tiny catapult I had thus made. Then I let my finger fly.

It was a perfect fillip that struck his nose hard. The shriveled body twitched and heaved. My brother turned from clay brown to clay red. He writhed, twisted, squirmed and thrashed. Then suddenly he coughed. There was a tiny shriek as he breathed in and a rattling cough as he spewed out a black ball made of phlegm and blood. Then his mouth opened very wide and he cried.

It was, from the beginning, a cry of rage. That much is true. As if he knew in that instant that exile would be his natural state. But as for not being born and coming into the world astride his charger, that was sheer self-deluding rhetoric.

He never thanked me for restoring his life to him though he learned about it very early from my mother, who never tired of telling him the miraculous story. No. Hans was not given to the gentler emotions: affection, gratitude, delight. His genius was of a different sort. Having nourished (and indulged in) the fancy that he was the wandering outlaw of his own dark mind, a being who was either not of this world or else that he was infinitely superior to it, his talents were of a different order: he could hold grudges, cherish vengeance, or inflict ingenious punishment.

He did not spare me his account of what he did to the saffron vendor.

"She was not hard to follow," he said. "Even after a week, the traces of her clumsy flight through our forest were easy to see. As I rode, I had to push wet branches aside that sometimes slapped at me.

"I rode from shadow to shadow, hearing the sound the folds of her skirt had made as she fled. I rode past three willow trees that overhung a pool. I heard an owl call from one of the willows. I would have ridden on, but my horse stopped at the sound. I listened and heard the owl say, 'You.'

"And there she was, sitting between a couple of great moss-covered roots of a flowering acacia tree. Above her, the fragrant yellow blossoms trembled. She sat, her face tear-stained and smudged, and ate gooseberries from a pile in her lap. The owl in the willow tree said, 'You.'

"I dismounted and stood over her. She looked up and tried to smile as if that would keep me from her. She trembled, already arranging her limbs to tell me, 'No.'

" 'Where is the Persian?' I said.

"Her eyes wide, she shook her head. I prodded her with the toe of my boot. 'Where is he?'

" 'I don't know. I've lost him.'

" 'You want him back?'

" 'Oh yes, I do.'

" 'And me? What about me?' I knelt beside her and pushed the hair out of her eyes.

" 'You are very beautiful,' she said. 'It would be sweet to love you.'

" 'You think that?' I said, standing again. You think that I am beautiful, and it would be sweet to love me?

" 'Yes, sir.'

" 'And the old man? What of him?'

" 'He woke me. He taught me.'

" 'What did he teach you?' I asked, raking one of her thighs with a spur.

" 'Ah, don't hurt me, prince.'

" 'What did he teach you?' I raked her other thigh.

" 'About love.'

" 'Fancy that. Did he teach you this?' I bent and tore away her bodice. Her breasts were startling white against the saffron color of her dress. I pinched one breast and then another.

" 'Oh no,' she begged.

" 'What did he teach you—about love?'

" 'He said,' she sobbed, 'that I have a name that some good man will hear when he grows dizzy at the sight of stars.'

" 'And this good man will come looking for you? Is that it?' I said as I prodded the triangle between her legs with the toe of my boot.

" 'Yes. Oh prince. How can you be both beautiful and cruel?'

" 'It is a gift from the gods. Tell me, does the old man do that? Does he do this? What does he tell you?'

" 'Stop, prince. Stop. Ah, prince, I beg you.'

" 'What does he tell you?'

" 'He says that there is sweetness in being young. That there is love in the world. That I must stay awake to find it. That I must learn to listen. That I must keep clean.'

" 'Then he paddles with his fingers, here, and here, and here? Isn't that so?'

" 'No, prince. No. Oh God, spare me . . .'

" 'He tells you, doesn't he, that you fill his dreams? That in the darkness of this world you are a light? The feminine principle that completes the creation?'

" 'Stop. Stop.' She clawed at me with her fingernails.

" 'But see what you are to me. A fuck. A stinking fuck. A cunt,' I said, 'that stinks of every swamp in Africa.'

"'Love,' she tried to say but I stopped her by doing what no woman could have borne. I lurched and there was a salt taste in my mouth as something broke. As she collapsed beneath me, I saw a shower of jagged crystal in her eyes before they closed. When I woke, I felt clammy and cold. I mounted my horse but before I rode off, I called out to her where she lay in the churned mud between two moss-covered roots of the acacia tree." 'Tell him. Be sure to tell him what else you know about love.'"

XXII

"YOU'RE crying," the harelip said.

I turned and shifted on his bed. "No," I lied. "It's just a trick of the moonlight. What with your story and my own reminiscences I may well have acquired a mournful look."

He ignored my explanation. "Have you noticed," he said, "that tears can be nourishing?"

I grunted but said nothing. I was too tired. I felt an ache in my shoulders brought on by the moon-drenched, cool night air. I shifted from side to side, trying to loosen my muscles, trying to push down whatever things were thrusting up at me from under the reed coverlet of the bed. I moved my tongue against the soft flesh of my lower jaw, hoping to squeeze some moisture into my mouth.

"I know about tears," the harelip said. "I am something of an adept at them."

"I see." I did not speak with conviction.

"You don't. You ought to cherish your tears."

"That doesn't mean I have to display them."

"Share. Not display. That's all I ever asked for."

"Please," I said impatiently. "Don't be insistent. I need some time to think. I'm tired . . . puzzled." I sank back into the reed coverlet and closed my eyes. After the memories I had just recalled, I wanted to hear every word of the story that Amalasuntha told me when we exchanged that long look of love as my handsome brother Hans was carrying her down from the glass mountain.

XXIII

"ONE day," she said, "my father crept into my room and sat on my Moroccan *pouf*, three yards from my bed. 'I'm afraid of you,' he said. 'I would not touch you for the world. You are my daughter. Why would I touch you?'

"That was after I was no longer a child.

"I must have had a childhood first in which I was fed and clothed. Someone took the trouble to bathe me; to teach me human habits. I think . . . or I dream . . . that a servant's child joined me in a corner for some play; that a nurse brushed my hair; that someone tall taught me the difference between A and B. I must have had a childhood, but when I try to seize its memories, they slide away. My father did not see me often, but when he did, he always mistook me for someone else.

"Then my body changed and he was surprised to notice that I was me. That the scalded, female thing whose untied umbilicus had sent him moaning from my mother's room was turning into a woman.

"The change was slow, but he hovered near to watch it, phase by phase. Feeling his eyes on me, I ran to the forest where he followed me on tiptoes. I tried to hide from him in caves, in groves of trees, in secret arbors.

"One day, I lay at the foot of a catalpa tree at the end of a natural corridor in the woods where shafts of light poured

141

down, warming the starch in my linen shirt. Slowly, I unbuttoned it. I lay on my back with my face in the shade and watched the light playing in the leaves. My hand was raised to my exposed breast, my finger all but touching my newly irritable nipple. Out of the corner of my eye, I caught a glimpse of my father peering at me from where he stood, pressed against the trunk of a nearby oak.

"I said, 'Nipple.' Like that: 'Nipple.' I could hear my father's fingernails scraping the bark of his tree. Under my hovering finger, there was more than the warmth of the sun. In my nostrils there was the smell of decomposing leaves, of blindworms moving under stones.

"I said, 'Nipple,' and giggled because it was that kind of word. I was thirteen. The year before I wouldn't have said it. Then there was nothing but a brown mark where now there was so much sunlight and pressure—and an ant moving confusedly over the mound of my breast. I felt my mouth fill with pleasure. I leaned back and pressed my head hard against the earth.

"The forest smelled of bark, of sunlight, of moist soil. I wondered, 'If I touch . . . if I guide the ant upward, which I will not do . . . will I need to turn in the direction of my father's tree?'

"A beam of sunlight crept under my closed eyelid and everything I saw was formless and golden. I raised my belly. I felt the sockets of deep bones unlock.

"The year before I was much older. Now, I was new. I breathed a stifling but delicious air. As I watched the hurrying ant, I felt a pressure in my throat of a delight on which I was afraid I would choke. With every moment that passed, I felt myself turning newer than before. I closed my eyes tightly.

"Even as I heard my father rubbing against his tree, I dreamed of a falcon falling in a gorge. A wounded falcon that fell out of a hot sky to strike the ledge on which a serpent rested. Its wings broken, its head bruised, the falcon dragged itself erect. The serpent stared at it, unmoved. Far below, in the gorge, a river cut through stone on its way to the sea.

"On its ledge, the serpent coiled into its folds. It looked up at the sky from which the bird had fallen, then across at the dying falcon. The bird dragged itself to the edge of the chasm and looked down. Though it would be mangled by boulders as it fell, there would finally be a clean, an easier, death waiting for it there, and a grave in the rushing waters of the river.

"Slowly, the snake uncoiled. The falcon inched back from the precipice. The snake's tongue flickered and its folds opened to the falcon that, dreaming the word 'easier,' entered them, its eyelids closed.

"I was suddenly cold. Flicking away the ant, I buttoned my shirt. My father, stealing away, stumbled on a log and sent a cloud of brilliant tiger butterflies fluttering into a shaft of sunlight.

"Behind me, I heard an owl munching at the only word it knew. 'Who?' it said. 'Who?' I heard the timorous mice quarreling for space beneath the oak against whose side my father had leaned.

"It was on that very night that my father crept into my room. He sat on my Moroccan *pouf* and held his palm out to me so I could see the broken ant he had retrieved. He said, 'Ah, Amy, Amy. You are my daughter. I would not dream of touching you.'

"A year passed while I roamed the forest by day and pretended, or thought I pretended, not to notice my father's eyes on me at night. He began to shave his mustache into a thinner, sharper line. When he passed me in a corridor, he waved a hand at me and said a strangled, 'Hello.'

"More frequently, he came into my room at night. He sat on my Moroccan *pouf* looking frail, diminished. He said, 'I would not touch you. You are my daughter. I would not touch you for the world.' From the narrow cot on which I lay, I watched him. He looked like an unused bow.

"He sighed. 'Ah, Amy. How sad I am.'

"'What is it?' I asked. I was not yet fourteen.

"Covering his face with his hands, he said, 'Oh, nothing. Nothing but the usual loneliness. My God. If you knew. It's like being a rock in a dead calm sea. Inert. Inert. Inert. And all I ask is a bit of unguarded affection. A touch of disinterested love.'

"He spread his fingers so I could see the glitter in his eyes as he gazed toward me. 'Daddy, don't be sad,' I told him.

"'Disinterested affection, that's all. But such a thing's not to be had nowadays. I am the king and no one will let me forget it. Advancement, promotion, interest. There's no such thing as pure affection. Who cares about trustworthy kisses? And oh, Amy, look. My hair is turning gray – at forty-two.'

"He came to my room even more frequently. Always, he hid his eyes with his hands, but always I could see them gleaming while he talked. As his speech flowed past me, I flexed the joints in my toes; I twisted my foot around and around my ankle; I wriggled my kneecaps and tested the muscles in my shoulders. Sometimes, I wiggled my ears.

"When he was gone, leaving the spray of his language still hovering in my room, I stared out at the night and thought about owls and foxes, of rabbits with their heads in snares. Then I thought of the strange shapes his words had shaken into the air: shadows engulfing shadows; dark concavities flowing on my white walls.

"One morning, I woke, feeling swollen, thick. I was fourteen years old. I crept from the castle and went to the forest where I knew a pool in which I liked to bathe. I was not frightened. I only wanted to feel less swollen, and cleaner, than I was. Under the icy water, I examined my body: my breasts, my slender waist, my full hips. I watched the shapes my long black hair made swirling in the pool. Like black ink in clear water. Then, mysteriously, the ringlets of black hair coiled and mingled with drifting streaks of pale red.

" 'So,' I thought. 'That is the end of my childhood.' And my mind welled with praises for the pool in which I had learned so much. It had been a friend to my childhood; it was my friend still, as it helped me to bathe away the signs of the moon. I did not feel sad for soiling its water. In less than half a day, it would be clear, and I would be able to drink from it again.

"I lay in the grass and watched a golden snail climb over a sun-warmed rock, leaving a trail of slime. I dipped my forefinger into the sticky stuff and rubbed it over the snail's warm shell. It drew in its horns and waited. After a while, the horns came out and the snail resumed its journey.

"I felt wonderful. It was lovely to be young and to feel new. When I put my hand to the crisp delta between my legs, I did not feel ashamed.

"I do not know whether my father guessed what had happened, but that night, when he came to my room, his voice seemed more compelled, more strident than it had ever been before. He was plaiting an invisible thong and, silently, I braided it with him. So long as I had not been ready, his hot tumble of language had not frightened me. Now, with the change in my body, I knew that if I did not drive him from my room, I would become his accomplice.

"I did not drive him from my room.

"I was fourteen years old. A maiden, no longer a girl. I let him talk because his voice was one more of the springtime voices that I heard now on every side: the whinnying of mares on distant mountains and the stallions whickering in reply; the high-pitched courtship of cats at midnight beside the courtyard well; the yelp of coupling dogs; and sows grunting under boars. My father's voice among all those others turned my lips dry, my breath hot.

"He sat on my Moroccan *pouf* and talked through his fingers. I, in my narrow trundle bed, gave off the lilac fragrance of youth; of starch and sunlight, soap and clear water. He smelled of ropes of sea-salt, of sweat and musk.

"'Lately,' he said, 'even the rabbits get away from me, let alone the deer. From me, the king.'

"I said, 'Tomorrow will be better.'

"'Amy, the woods are full of game. I *know* the deer are standing in the underwood beside the trail. I can hear their teeth snapping at low branches. I can hear them scratching their backsides against the trees.'

"'Another time,' I said. 'Another time.' My fingers pressed against the sides of my bed. My shoulders ached.

"'Amy! The boar trots out to greet me. He rubs his crippled tusk against an oak and waits for me to shoot. He says, "How do you do?" Amy, he bows before me, and when I shoot, he's gone. Why, Amy?'

"'Hunter's luck,' I said. 'It will change.'

"'No. Animals can smell failure. The rabbits—the very rabbits despise me.'

"'What does a rabbit know?' I said, passing my tongue over my lips.

"'It's because I'm lonely. They know I'm lonely. I lumber through the forest pushing loneliness before like a barrow.'

"I did not hear him. I was thinking, 'Three times now the pool has been stained, and three times it has been clear.' I passed my hands over my sides.

"'Amy,' my father said. 'Am I wicked?'

"'How do I know? How can I tell?' Outside my window the moonlight gleamed like newly fallen snow.

"'No. It can't be that I am wicked. But a man like me . . . with so much on my mind. Such heavy responsibilities. A man like me needs serenity. I require reassurance. Even a king needs reassurance. A woman could reassure me.'

"From my bed, my eyes fixed on the moon. I said, 'I am no longer a girl.'

"My father stared at my moonwashed bed. He chewed the corners of his mustache. Between us, the silence was thick with the shapes of what I half knew and what he could not bring himself to acknowledge. All his sentences had brought him to this point. I was his daughter. I might be a woman. One final time, I heard him say, 'I would not touch you for the world. What would you think of me?'

"As if I were talking to the moonlight, I said, 'You are my father.' Then I lay still and waited, my swollen lower lip between my teeth.

"I did not fall in love with him. He did not fall in love with me. My bed was narrow. There was a long, long pause before he crossed the room."

XXIV

"MY father and I were not a loving couple. Having taken my virginity with the gaping eagerness of a man who has leaped from a cliff, he lay beside me, amazed that there had been room for us both in my narrow bed.

"It was he who had cried out. I minded the pain, but not much. He, when he was done, fell back and waited for lightning to strike him. He lay, his lips blue. I thought, 'There's something wrong. This can't be all there is.' A thin seepage of blood crept down my thigh.

"So, I moved. After all that sunshine and the teasing pressure of my back and head against the moist earth; after the sunbeams in my eyes and the throaty voices from the undergrowth; after the bird song and the animal cries and my father's leering behind the oak tree, was I meant to lie there like a breathing log? Was all that waiting to end in a twinge in the dark; a rude poke that made me bleed?

"I moved. Young as I was, I knew he owed me something more than a display of terror. More than his frantic, 'Amy! Amy! What have I done?'

"'Not very much,' I almost said. 'Not much.' The bed was narrow and I was young and full of energy. It was he who had crossed the room, who had entered my bed. My eyes had widened but they had not closed. My skin was flushed, my blood turgid, my body arched. This was no time for him to be playing Wickedness Appalled. And so I moved.

"I moved. I turned. I confronted my father thigh to thigh. 'Amy,' he groaned, 'what are we doing? Amy! Amy!'

"I growled. I moved. I squirmed. Something else was owed to me. I reached and tore. My body's warmth and smell filled the tiny cave my sheet made over us. I moved. He caught his tongue between his teeth.

"There was a long silence. The stars creaked in their courses. I heard the gnawing wash of old oceans against pebbled shores. If my father would not teach me, my blood would. I twined and churned, scraping bone against bone. I hissed, I scratched, I bit.

"We were on a pebbled shore beside a grinding sea. Behind us, there were caves through which jets of salt rolled from one dark pool to another. Something tossed us high, high. There was an instant of bewildered joy; an uproar of the senses; moist hair and fingertips; drowned odors, hoarse sounds. A great crash, followed by the long, slow ebbing of ecstasy, followed by an obliterating sleep.

"From which I woke, young, curious, healthy, energetic and alert. My father lay beside me like an emptied snail shell. 'Oh God,' he sobbed. 'My God, what have we done? Amy, Amy! Ah my darling, that was good.'

"That was the beginning of the glass mountain. But before that came to pass, he braided his flesh with mine.

"'A man,' he often whispered, 'a man in his daughter's bed is a link out of the human chain.'

"'Yes,' I said, and moved another way he did not know.

"'Oh God, Amy, what are you doing now?' he said to my pillow while his fingers followed my instruction.

"'I'll die,' he groaned. 'Oh darling, I'll die.'

"'Die tomorrow,' I said between gritted teeth. 'Now, *move*.'

"Night after night, he stumbled into my room like a newly blinded man and dragged himself from the Moroccan *pouf* to the window and then back to the door. I lay in my schoolgirl's bed and counted stars. I knew to the fraction of a second how much time would elapse before he joined me in my bed. His tongue and teeth chirred like an aviary.

"There were times when I would not let him come into my room. Then, I put fresh sheets on my bed, cleared the room of anything that was his and slept alone, testing if I could feel again like the swollen girl who had lain beneath the flowering catalpa and watched the ant circling her nipple.

"It did not work. My bed was clean and my room was quiet and I had braided my hair in schoolgirl braids. I lay on my back, my hands folded over my breasts, doing what I could to make myself look as nearly like a waiting virgin as I could.

"It didn't work. Time was against me, and knowledge. What the body learns, it cannot unlearn, and so, feeling a tingle at my breast, or some deeper yearning, I whistled. My father, waiting at the door, came tumbling to my bed.

"He was lonely. He had dreamed of kisses freely given; of disinterested, reassuring love. But from the moment he became my lover, all the other patterns of his life became irrelevant. He was neither strong enough nor astute enough to balance more than one set of contradictions at a time. When he meant to be paternal, he was lecherous; when he reached for his mistress, he discovered his daughter's head against his shoulder. 'It's forbidden,' he cried, even as his nerves hummed at the convolutions we achieved. 'What are we doing?'

"When he woke in the morning, drained and slack, he sat on the edge of my bed, his nightshirt not quite covering his knees, and tried to be a father to me. In the light of day, he averted his eyes, keeping them fixed on one or another of the iron claws of my bed. 'Well,' he asked in his hearty, would-be manly fashion, 'how are things? I mean, things in general.'

"I, who liked the mornings even less than he, was irritated. 'You know very well how things are,' I snapped.

"He put his face between his hands and said, 'Yes. Of course. I mean . . . I mean, you know . . . Are you all right? That sort of thing. That is, do you have what you need? Clothes? Earrings? Money?'

" 'I'm your daughter,' I said, 'not your whore.'

" 'Don't,' he pleaded. 'I was just trying to be . . . '

" 'Paternal? Lover-like?'

" 'I am your daddy, after all . . . '

" 'Yes, Daddy,' I said. 'Yes, Daddy.'

I was not always spiteful. There were times between the storm winds of the night when I felt rising in me an ordinary impulse to quiet with love the man who lay beside me. If my blood had ancient sensual secrets hidden in it, it had its share of less stormy wisdom too. A vision plucked at the edges of my consciousness of a woman holding her husband's head in her lap, rubbing his temples with her fingertips. It was a wistful idea, but it had as much authority as the instincts that guided our embraces. I looked at him, sleeping, and, forgetting who he was, I longed to soothe, to calm, to be fond of my man. I wanted to lie beside him, glad of the rhythm his breathing made. I wanted the pleasure of coming inadvertently upon some article of his clothing and pressing it against my nose. I wanted indulgent memories of his bad jokes and his ineptitudes.

"I wanted something healing and ordinary . . . but as I mused, he woke and reached for me and we raged and pounded the night away.

"The months passed. The servants, acting on intuition or guilty knowledge, added softer furniture to my room. There was a painted camel-skin lamp on my bedside table that gave off a muted red, green and yellow light. A rug, bought from a soothsaying Persian who passed through the kingdom, brightened my floor. On my bed there was a hand-embroidered coverlet with a tiger-butterfly design.

"I was fourteen years old, inexhaustibly energetic. I neither knew nor could imagine that there were years ahead of me; that there was an entire lifetime to be lived. For my father, who was a prisoner of his confusions, and for myself, who was supremely ignorant, there was something silken and seductive in living only for one's senses. Then one night, at the very summit of an ecstasy, it occurred to me that one could live at the utmost pitch of excitement only with a stranger, and then only for a very short time. For solace, for happiness, there had to be some exchange of selves.

"As my father slept, I got out of bed and went to the table from which I took the painted camel-skin lamp. I lighted it and turned its wick very low. With the lamp in my hand, I went silently back toward the bed and stood beside it, letting the light soften the outlines of my father's face. I wanted to see him once without distraction. Just to *see* the man my body knew. To see if I could recognize him.

"He lay in a shallow sleep. His neatly trimmed mustache that could look so fierce and martial when he was in his royal uniform looked silly now that his face was relaxed.

"A nerve in his left eyelid pulsed, frightening me. My hand shook. I watched as the eyelid that had trembled was drawn upward. For a moment I stared into his eye and saw that the iris surrounded the pupil like an obsidian ring. There, inside the eye, there was a diminutive version of myself holding the lamp. My long black hair seemed to be swirling in a pool. I saw the gash my father had made in the right sleeve of my nightgown and I had a slovenly view of my exposed breast. Then the sight of tears welling up in his eye startled me so my hand shook. A drop of oil from the lamp fell on his forehead. I watched as his eye closed. I shuddered and blew out the lamp.

"Nothing else happened just then. At the same time, I knew that I could not get back into my bed with him. For the rest of the night, I lay curled like a kitten on the Moroccan *pouf*. Frequently, I heard my father groan but he did not wake until long past dawn. When he did, he sat up in bed and shook his head as if he were trying to rid himself of a persistent fly. Then he got out of bed and looked around. He saw me crouched on the *pouf* like a child with the bellyache and came over to me. He lifted my chin and said uncertainly, 'Amy, dear. I've had the most terrible dream.'

" 'What is it?' I asked

" 'I dreamed . . .' he began, but then the pain of the oil hit him. He shrieked and ran from the room, but not before I had time to see the round gleaming silver pit the drop of spilled oil had seared in his forehead."

XXV

"THE silver wound on my father's forehead would not heal. It was not unsightly, and at first I actually thought that it improved his looks, because it gave to his dark features a certain elegant hauteur, as if he had acquired the caste mark of a rajah. But the mark was painful. From the moment the drop of oil hit his skin, he was always in one or another degree of torment. Sometimes the pain subsided into a dull throbbing, at other times his screams lacerated the sky as he succumbed to what seemed like an onslaught of whirling drills against his skull.

"Eventually, even the worst of his pain became part of a rhythm to which he became accustomed. His mien, taught by suffering, became more manly and his manner ironical.

"I thought he would see his wound as the punishment he had so long been expecting and that it would keep him from my bed. Instead, three weeks after the accident with the lamp, there he was, in the doorway of my room. When I drew back, he smiled and said, 'Come Amy. Now that we know the punishment, we might as well enjoy the crime.'

" 'Enjoy?'

"He unbuttoned his doublet.

"And now began a new period of avidity. Where he had been frightened and obedient, he was now a hot dry force, invading me night after night. His teeth clenched, his eyes wide open, he moved above me silently, indifferent to any mood or feeling of my own. Whatever he did, he did over and over again. When, after the longest time, he achieved his spasm it was joyless, searing, dry.

"Since the appearance of the silver mark, my father could not sweat, with the result that his skin, no matter what his exertions, gave off an odor of vellum. His lips acquired a thin plasticity; his breath was hot and pungent. Once, as he labored over me, I looked up and saw granules of pain streaming like insects through the tiny blood vessels in his eyes. 'He's going to die,' I thought. 'Soon, he's going to die.'

"He seemed to know it, too. He lost weight; his skin turned ashen; he tottered when he walked. One morning, in a cool moment after dawn, when his eyes, for an instant, had lost their feverish glitter, he sat up in my bed and said, 'This can't go on, Amy. I'll have to go to her.' He caught his breath.

"I was silent and waited, unwilling to say the words that, with a man's cowardice, he wanted me to say for him. Finally, he said, 'I hurt, Amy. I can't bear it any longer. I'll have to go to her . . . ' He put his hand out, like an orphan begging for alms.

"I kept still. If he meant to go to the Witch of the Wood, the decision, and the words, would have to be his.

"He talked to my silence, justifying, explaining. 'Oh God, Amy. There's the pain. And there's you. I know what she'll do. She'll make me give you up, and I can't bear that. But I can't bear the pain either. And I can't bear . . . ' he waved an arm to indicate our bed. He leaned toward me and put his hand on my shoulder. 'Do you hear me, Amy? Do you understand?'

"I know I was supposed to feel pity. I was expected to say, 'Yes, of course. Go to her. She is a healer. She will end your suffering.' I said nothing.

"There began, then, a long month in which these pathetic scenes were repeated. More than once, sheer exasperation rather than pity prompted me to cry, 'Oh for God's sake go to her,' but the words stuck in my throat. On that first night, he had, after all, crossed the room of his own accord. And why should *he* be healed, since there was no healing anywhere in sight for me?

"And then . . . After all, I was just fifteen years old. However bleak our lives had become, he was all the father and all the lover I had. If he meant to leave me, I wanted him to act responsibly. So, I withheld my pity and let my robe fall open.

"Finally, accident resolved the matter. Lately, as if he were challenging fate to intervene in his life, he had taken to riding through the forest at dusk at breakneck speed without using either bridle or stirrups. He sat in the saddle humped low, like an ape, risking overhanging branches and thorns, goading his horse with sweeps of his spurs. On the evening of which I speak, his horse, maddened by a particularly cruel thrust of the spurs, flung itself against a tree and fell, sending my father tumbling into the dust.

"When he stopped rolling, he found he was lying in the open space before the Witch's cave. Beside him, not inches from where he lay, there was a tethered nanny goat that eyed him with distaste. The Witch herself rose from a small fire she was tending and came to him.

"She was a tall dark Lapp woman whose weight was all hard flesh. Her smooth grey hair, bound in a single gold thread, hung in well-oiled braids to her waist. Her face was broad, her forehead wide. Her eyes, under thick brows that met in the middle, were deep brown, soft, alert. Her large nose was molded rather than chiseled, but her mouth was well-formed, her lips full. To my father, slightly stupefied by his fall, she was an apparition, somewhat oversized, but congenial and warm.

"She knelt beside him and took his head into her hands and settled it on a pile of sheep shearings she scooped from a nearby basket. 'And how is your Majesty?' she asked. Still stunned and breathless from his fall, he said nothing. She stroked his temples and rubbed his neck and seemed to mutter spells. When he was thoroughly relaxed, she settled his head against the sheep shearings and went back to stirring her kettle. He thought she looked very well there, sitting straight-backed in her blue silk tunic, her legs crossed under her while the glow of the fire cast a warm light on her face.

"When she deemed the time was right, she poured broth from her kettle into an olive wood cup and carried it to him. She lifted him to a sitting position and held him against her shoulder. She put the cup to his lips and he sipped. As he drank, his eyes began to lose their glaze.

"With the warm pressure of her arm around him, he looked into her brown eyes and heaved a sigh. Again she brought the cup to his lips. Though the broth was hot, he drank greedily. When he was done, he made no effort to move out of the comforting embrace.

" 'Now,' she said, 'roll over.' Without a murmur, he did what he was told. She knelt beside him and put her large hands under his shirt and rubbed his shoulders, making powerful thrusts over the soft muscles in his back. From his shoulders, her hands moved down to his waist. He lay, his cheek on the palm of one hand, looking into her firelight. 'Thank you,' he whispered. 'Thank you.'

" 'Shall I do it some more?'

" 'Yes, oh please, yes.'

"She smiled and continued the movements of her strong hands. After a while she said, 'That's enough. Now, sit up.'

"He obeyed, savoring a pleasure that went well beyond the effects of her massage. At first, he could not identify what it was, then, putting his hand to his forehead, he understood. 'It doesn't hurt,' he said. 'Oh, it has been hurting for the longest time.'

"She put a brown finger on the silver mark and said, 'It's still there. So long as you are in the precincts of my cave, it won't hurt. When you leave . . . '

"He closed his eyes. Taking her hand, he said, 'What must I do? Tell me, please.'

"She bent and put her lips to the silver mark. Her breath was like warm milk. 'Don't talk,' she said. 'Rest, now.'

"He fell asleep at once. When he woke, he learned that a night and a day had passed, but the Witch of the Wood was still beside him, still holding his hand. He looked up into her face and said, 'Oh, I feel good,' and fell promptly asleep again. When he woke the following evening, he felt sublimely rested. Her silk blue tunic was smooth against his cheek.

" 'I've slept and slept and slept!' he said.

" 'Yes.'

" 'I haven't slept . . . Oh, it's been so long. That mark. The pain . . . '

" 'Yes,' she said. 'It will hurt again.'

" 'When I leave here.'

" 'Yes.'

" 'And there's no way to end it?'

"She rose and went to the fire from which she returned bringing a dish of meat from which she fed him, morsel by delicious morsel. When he was done, she wiped his mouth with a scrap of clean linen and piled more sheep shearings under him so that he lay as on a couch.

" 'My daughter,' he began. 'My daughter troubles my sleep.'

" 'Yes?'

" 'We make the nights haggard.'

" 'Yes?'

"Then, angrily, 'It was *she* who spilled the oil . . . '

" 'And you, . . . what did you spill?'

" 'No,' he cried. 'It wasn't my fault. I saw her in the pool. I saw her lying in her bed. She taunted me. She flaunted herself.'

" 'She did not make you cross the room.'

" 'Yes. Yes, she did.'

" 'No, your Majesty. You first, and then she, have turned each other into two arcs of the same hoop.'

" 'But I'm the one who can't sleep, who can't rest, and whose forehead burns . . . '

"She was implacable. 'Two arcs of the same hoop. Break the hoop.'

" 'How?' he pleaded. " 'How?'

"Abruptly she said, 'Are you in love with your daughter?'

" 'Ah, God. How do I know? I am . . . I am . . . No. Not in love.' Tears spurted to his eyes. 'I want not to feel

that damned vibration in my loins. I don't . . . I don't want
to cross the room. I don't want to stop crossing the room.'
He pressed his head against her lap. 'Help me. Help.'

" 'Hush,' she said as she stroked his hair. 'Hush. You are
a king. You can also be a man.'

"He beamed with pleasure at the lie: He was a king
and he could be a man. Then, some worm of integrity
stirred in his brain prompting him to sit up. He looked into
her soft brown eyes and said, 'You don't understand. I am
very wicked.'

" 'Probably not.'

" 'There is my daughter . . . '

" 'More of that, later.'

" 'I have loathsome thoughts.'

" 'No doubt.'

" 'You don't understand. I have . . . even before Amy.
Before she was born. I have not only thought ugly things. I
have done them.'

" 'Yes.'

" 'No. Listen. I must tell you.'

" 'Tell, if you must.'

" 'Always. Even when I was very young. Always, behind
my eyes, I lived in a puff of bad air where I rolled in a dark
shed, unbuttoned, itching, exhausting myself on phantoms.'

" 'Dreams,' she murmured. 'Bad dreams.'

" 'Ah, how I wish they were. I have been to Baghdad
where I have seen, and done, the unspeakable.'

" 'Who has not? We are alive. We endlessly endeav-
or love.'

" 'No,' he cried. 'You don't understand. In Baghdad,
there was no question of love.'

" 'There is always a question of love.'

" 'No,' he insisted. 'Not in Baghdad. Let me tell you . . .'

" 'Tell,' she said. 'Tell if you must.'

" 'In Baghdad . . . oh, what a foul city. Onions and lice. Tangerines and piss. The men are tall, muscular; the women heavy, full-bodied. Both are dark and untrammeled. There is nothing they will withhold.'

" 'People. Men and women, doing what they can.'

" 'No, they are bred and trained to disorder the senses. They touch . . . they . . . '

" 'Caress . . . '

" 'Not they,' he insisted. 'Their touch is loathsome, exciting beyond the power of flesh to endure.'

" 'The Witch of the Wood cradled his head. 'Hush,' she said. 'There are mistaken kisses; unhappy embraces; cruelties in love. But the desire for union is deep in the bone.'

" 'Repulsive,' he cried. 'Repulsive. Listen. One of their women found me there in a *kuchi*. I had been misdirected and I was dazed and fatigued. She greeted me in the dark. A woman as tall and as handsome as you. She gave me her right hand to hold while with her left, she plucked at her veil, letting me have a glimpse in the lamplight of her moist lips. I clung to her dirty hand and followed where she led.

" 'We crossed a courtyard littered with debris. There was a thin sliver of a moon in the sky shedding an uncertain light on the sleepy barn fowl we passed, and on low dunghills.

" 'Then all at once we were in a corridor that smelled of cumin and piss. Unseen creatures bit my ankles. I felt myself growing alert. Eager for . . . something.

" 'We entered a room without windows that was lighted by a single lamp. It was a white-washed room with no other furniture in it but a chair that faced a low stage. The tall woman, my guide, asked me to sit in the chair, after which she kissed my cheek and ran her tongue into my ear. Then she was gone.

"'I was left sitting there in what I understood to be a tiny theater. I sat and waited, and watched the shadows made by the lamplight playing on the wall. A child's voice nearby whispered, "Dear Sir, no one has ever left this house unfulfilled. No matter what strange notions . . . no matter how forbidden . . . Here, the dream is made flesh . . . "

"'I sat with my hands in my lap. Around me, the small theater was lapped in shadows. Suddenly, there was a thumping sound as two naked young women appeared bearing lighted candelabra which they set down, one on each side of the stage. They disappeared, only to return again, this time harnessed to a cart on which there was a structure that looked like a giant bird cage made of straps of metal. Inside the cage stood a gigantic man, naked except for a belt from which there hung a dagger in an embroidered scabbard. His arms were outstretched and his wrists were clamped in bracelets of brass.

"'The women drew the cart to one end of the stage, then they disappeared only to return with a second cart in which, again, there stood a manacled naked man, armed, like the first, with a dagger in an embroidered scabbard hanging from the belt around his waist. The women withdrew leaving the naked manacled men face to face. At first, they stared, simply puzzled.

"'I too was puzzled. From somewhere left of the stage, there came the sound of brass bells, and now the two naked women came back, leading a third woman between them.

She was simply magnificent. Her hair was long and black, her waist narrow and her hips were slim. Though the women leading her were naked and she was clothed in a long gown of the sheerest silk, she emanated an erotic heat that tormented the men in their cages even as it tormented me. The naked women put the clothed beautiful one between the two cages and left the stage.

"'And now, I saw that the cages were no longer firmly set on the stage. That by means of a pulley arrangement, each of the cages was rising into the air. When they were both a foot or two above the floor, the cages began to move in an ellipse around the woman, who slowly commenced to dance. The men in their cages, their mouths open, breathed hard and strained at their manacles. Each of them endeavored to speak, but the sounds they made were sad evidence that they were mutes.

"The cages moved around her. The light on her gown shimmered over the movement of her breasts as she danced to the sound of the bells offstage. Her movements were graceful, but supremely naive as if she were only half aware of the meaning of her motions. Meanwhile, the cages moved around her, each cage now swinging closer to her and then away. With each swing, the frenzy of the man-acled men increased. By now, a rhythm had been estab-lished: desire for her, hatred for each other, separation. Desire, hatred, separation. The men sputtered, squeaked, gibbered.

"'The woman danced between the cages which now no longer moved in an ellipse around her. Instead, they swung toward each other each time that she slipped between them and clashed, at first lightly, then with increasing force. The

bells offstage rang; there was a tremendous sound of collid-
ing brass. The cages rebounded from their collision and
struck the floor of the stage and the mutes, their manacles
fallen from their wrists, the doors of their cages suddenly
open, stared for an instant at each other.

" 'I, the sole audience in that dark theater, seeing their
distended manhood, felt myself growing immense. I flour-
ished. I grew. I rose out of that thick darkness and swelled
past roof and rafter. I was sheer tumescence climbing
toward the sky. For a moment, I thought, "Where is she for
whom this tower is rising?"

" 'Then the enraged mutes leaped. There was a great
clattering of metal; the sound of silk tearing; a high-pitched
grunt. On stage, one of the mutes was on one knee, the
shaft of a dagger deep in his throat. The other, his arm flung
around the woman, was at his ecstasy. Both men had the
same look in their eyes while I, envying them both, roared
as the proud immensity between my legs exploded. The
light on stage failed, but not before I knew the full vastness
of the thrust with which I sent my sperm into the galaxies
where, I was certain, it would overwhelm the stars.' "

XXVI

"'CAN you blame me for thinking I am loath-some?' my father said.

"'The Witch of the Wood passed a hand through his hair. 'Hush,' she said. 'You were unhappy.'

"'I was there. I overwhelmed the stars. It was repulsive. Wonderful.'

"'Hush,' she said. Putting her fingers to his eyes, she sent him into another long, dreamless sleep.

"When he woke for the third time, he was lying in her dark cave. A clay oil lamp in which there floated a guttering wick cast a dim light. He struggled to his feet and looked around for the Witch and found her asleep on a mat near the entrance to the cave. Her body was bent as if her hands and feet had been tied together but the look on her broad Lapp face was restful. She looked warm and spent. She looked so comfortable that he got down on his hands and knees and pressed himself against her the way a piglet might against a sow from which it was nursing. Indeed, feeling him snuggling against her she grunted. He raised his arm and put it over her shoulder. She stirred and he felt her large bulk flowing over him. Her sleepy voice was in his ear. 'Stay with me. I need a king to love.' He burrowed closer against her and let his breath match the rhythmic rise and fall of her undemanding breasts. His

167

hands moved to touch them and he thought, 'How deep! How comfortable.'

" 'I need a king,' she said, her voice rich and sleepy.

" 'I am a king,' he replied. 'What are you?'

" 'A woman,' she said proudly. Her warmth was all over him. He felt his body dissolve and smiled.

"He put his tongue to her ear; his hand moved over her body. His touch produced no fever; he felt no haste. Only warmth and the smell of clean skin. 'Why,' he asked, amazed, 'why am I happy? What are you giving me?'

" 'Affection,' she said out of her sleep. 'The usual gift.' The melody of her breath flowing past his ear was like the distant humming of a breeze.

" 'Help me,' he said.

" 'Hold me,' she whispered as if the dream she was having were as pleasing as his own.

" 'Do I dare?' he asked.

" 'Why not? I am a woman.'

" 'Not a girl! Not a twist of lightning in the dark. Not Amalasuntha.'

"She stiffened. Something was wrong. It seemed to him that he had been wrapped like a pupa in a clean cocoon in which he had dreamed that the Witch of the Wood was beautiful, and now that dream had been made to spin to its end. His eyes tightly closed, he passed his hand over her face. His fingertips touched wrinkled leather cheeks, warts, moles, pits.

"To stop the unwinding of the dream cocoon, he said, 'Darling,' but the warmth in which he was immersed faded abruptly. His fingertips told him that her eyes were open.

He made an effort to kiss her, but his lips touched a knob on her upper lip and he drew back.

"Convulsively, he began to kick his way out of the dream cocoon; away from her enveloping flesh. From somewhere deep in his stomach, his hollow voice rose, 'You are ugly,' and he heard her say, 'Make me beautiful.'

"He sat up and opened his eyes and found her sitting beside him, watching him closely. He, in turn, tried to study her face but its details escaped him. There were wens and warts. There were no wens or warts. She smiled; she did not smile. Struggling to his feet, he smoothed his trim military mustache and said, 'Well. I'm afraid I woke you.'

"'More yourself than me,' she replied.

"'Did I say . . . have I promised anything?'

"'No.'

"'I did not violate . . .' he began. "'We did not by chance . . . ?'

"'No. Not by any chance. You have eaten and slept. Beyond that, you have done nothing.'

"He shook his head, trying to remember. 'I came to you . . . for help.'

"'Yes.'

"'You know why.'

"'You have a daughter.'

"'She torments me.'

"'You torment each other.'

"'But the pain is all mine.'

"'How do you know? Have you asked her?'

"'Why would I ask her? Look,' he pointed to the silver mark. 'That's on *my* forehead, not hers.'

"'Do you love her?'

" 'I told you. I feel hunger. I feel compelled. Parched.'

" 'She ought to be loved.'

" 'Woman! Can't you understand?' He thrust his finger into the now quiescent wound in his forehead. 'See. This is what it's all about. She is my daughter and a man in his daughter's bed is a link out of the human chain.'

" 'She needs to be loved.'

" 'She is my daughter,' he raved.

" 'Softly,' the Witch said. 'Someone must love her. Give her up.'

" 'To another *man?*'

" 'To all other men.'

"He leaned toward her. 'To be touched, nibbled, clawed, fondled, mounted.'

" 'To be loved. Offer her to be loved.'

" 'To a man who will stroke and pet and bite . . . '

" 'Who will love her.'

"He waited and waited and waited. Then he lifted his eyes, struggling unsuccessfully to hide the slyness in them. 'Very well,' he said. 'I will offer her to be loved.'

" 'By?'

" 'By men. By all other men.'

" 'You swear this?'

" 'I swear.'

"She looked narrowly at him. 'If you have sworn in bad faith, you will become your own revenge. If you have truly sworn, the mark, and the pain, will leave you.' Then, speaking carefully, delicately, she said, 'You could avoid it all. Your oath, the loss, the jealousy. You could stay here, with me. I need a king to love.'

"My father smiled. In the tone of a man who has just

concluded an excellent bargain, he said, 'Madame, you've been a great help to me. If you'll tell me what I owe you for your services, I'll be more than happy . . . '

"She said, 'Your Majesty is mistaken. I am a witch, not a whore.' Then she felled him with a blow of her fist. He found himself outside the cave not half a yard from the tethered nanny goat. For a while, he stayed where he was, on all fours, and tried to shake the dizziness from his head. Out of the corner of his eye, he saw the nanny goat drawing her hind legs up. A wave of nausea moved from his head to his stomach and back again. He saw no more of the goat until her iron hoof sent him flying against the roots of a catalpa tree where he landed with a cruel thump. For a long while, he lay there, too weak to move. It was there that his horse found him. It was with difficulty that he clambered into the saddle. Though he took up the reins, he had no notion where he was. Gratefully, he yielded all decision to his horse, which, trotting slowly, took him home.

"There, when he looked into his bedroom mirror, he saw that the silver mark was gone. Though he was still panting, he smiled. 'An oath,' he gloated. 'There must be more than one way to keep an oath.' Then he fell into his bed where he slept a dream-filled sleep.

XXVII

HERE, Amalasuntha's story, to which all the while I had been silently listening, was interrupted by a hoarse cry from the harelip. "You. Fat man. Are you listening? I've been talking to you." I looked up and saw the greedy light of authorship in his eyes.

"Of course I'm listening," I said.

"I have the feeling you're asleep."

"Then you have the wrong feeling."

"But something is wrong, isn't it?" He wrung his hands like a murderer who is regretting the life he is about to take. "You don't really care about anything I've said."

"Please," I said. "Isn't it enough that I've been listening? Don't try to gauge the degree of my sympathy, too."

"Given your silence, how can I gauge anything?" he said, his voice rising angrily.

To mollify him, I resorted to flattery. "I'm silent because your story is so engrossing. Why don't you go on?"

"Engrossing, eh? Oh, how fine it would be if you really thought so. You really want me to go on?"

"Yes," I lied. What did I care if he babbled? I knew what I knew. I was who I was. And yet, where did the twinge of sympathy come from that made me pass my hand over my upper lip to reassure myself that it was whole? And why did I pat my sides to make sure that they were fat. Before I could be sure of the answers, he had recommenced his tale.

But even as I listened to his story of the miller's daughter, another, a larger section of my mind was remembering the clear autumn morning when my brother Hans and I crossed the high mountains bordering Amalasuntha's kingdom and started down the highway that led to her capital. The road wound its way through clusters of pine trees whose crushed needles perfumed the air. On the far side of the valley we were skirting, there loomed the mountain of glass, a single, mile-high crystal that looked as if a waterfall had been shaped into a teardrop of the most lucid ice.

As I rode behind my brother, I found myself considering a new and very surprising thought. All the while we had been travelling together, I had taken for granted that when we came to the glass mountain, Hans would get Amalasuntha. But now I wondered, "Suppose I got her." Thus far, she had proved out of reach of everyone who had ridden for her. But the mountain did not play favorites. It was built to gratify only one successful rider and to disappoint all the others. Fate would choose the rider who got her. Neither horsemanship, nor the habit of success, nor good looks would insure triumph on the unclimbable glass. I was so stirred by these thoughts that I actually said aloud, "Hans! Just think. What if I get Amalasuntha?"

Hans, looking splendid in the saddle of his prancing black destrier, cast me a contemptuous look. "You? Don't be a ninny. Test the proposition on your tongue: 'Klaus, a feckless tub of lard, riding a spavined mare up a mile-high mountain of glass got to the top and embraced Amalasuntha, the most beautiful woman in the world.' No. No. It's not a sentence that history can accommodate."

"You don't know," I persisted. "What if Amalasuntha and I turn out to be destined for each other?"

"Ha!" he said, but I could see that the word 'destiny' irked him and I was glad. I liked what I had imagined, and, as the sunlight warmed me, I lulled myself with the thought that it was not impossible that I might point my mare against the glass and, with the ease of absolute innocence, ride her to the top of the glass mountain. I licked my lips with a greedy tongue. As I rode, my mare poured my flesh from side to side.

At a turn in the road, we came out into open country and looked down on a frost-bitten countryside. Below us, to our right, we could see wood smoke rising from the chimneys of the hovels that dotted the slope of our mountain. The shooks of the gathered harvest stood stiffly to attention in the ploughed fields in which flocks of starlings gleaned.

It was as we came abreast of a stand of beech trees just to our left that we heard a noise halfway between a growl and a whine. Hans reined in his nervous animal. I put my hand on my dagger and checked my mare. The noise that had caught our attention turned now into a rapid series of snuffles, yelps and sobs. At a nod from Hans, I dismounted and dropped my reins. Leaving my obedient mare, I waddled toward the cluster of beeches.

I had hardly entered the dappled shade when I stumbled on a rotten branch and nearly fell. At my outcry, Hans followed me into the clearing where we both paused amazed. There was the Persian, bent like a horseshoe, and struggling to free his beard from a cleft in the log on which he was crouched. The old man kicked with his thin legs and waved his arms weakly like an inverted beetle.

Hans dismounted and tied his horse to a sapling. "Well," he said, "so it's you." Overhead and all around us, there was birdsong and the noise of chattering squirrels.

The old man, unable to lift his head, thrust one leg out behind him, like a dog making water, and peered up at my brother through the sweaty strands of hair hanging over his eyes. "Ah, prince," he began, trying to make a bow as he spoke, "it is I. Yes. Oh yes."

Ludicrous though he looked, he enticed pity, too. All of his old grace was gone. His eyes were red-rimmed, his throat was hoarse; he was barefooted and his rags were foul. But, though he hung over the log like a puppet half of whose strings had been cut, he was not entirely abject. Somewhere between his strong teeth, and in the light that still shone in his weary eyes, there lingered a vestige of his dignity.

Hans prodded the old man's ribs delicately with the toe of his boot. "In trouble, are you? Now, that's interesting." A rabbit thumped the ground nearby. A bluejay sent a raucous challenge to a shrike.

The Persian twisted his head around. "Yes. I am. Don't just gloat. Help me."

"I'll do it. Let me . . . " I blurted, starting forward.

"Stay," said Hans, thrusting me easily to one side. In the underbrush, grasshoppers and cicadas chirred. Hans knelt beside the old man and tweaked his beard.

"Oh! Oh! Stop it, prince. That hurts."

"Yes. I thought it might."

"Horribly."

"Leave him alone. Here, let me. I'll fix it . . . " I leaned
forward to cut the beard loose with my dagger.

Tears sprang to the Persian's eyes, "No, Klaus. Don't
kill me with your kindness. My locks are blessed. If you cut
one hair, I am a dead man."

"Then how . . . ?" I started to say, but Hans pushed
me aside.

"I know how," Hans snapped. Turning to the Persian
he said, "Listen to me, necromancer. I will free you from
this log—"

"Ah, Hans. Would you? Can you? How good you are.
How kind." The Persian's tears coursed down his nose.

Hans said coldly, "Neither the one nor the other. What
I do is for my own sake."

"Excellent, prince. Clear-eyed. The way of the world.
But, oh Lord, hurry."

"He hates you, old man," I whispered. "Don't let him
touch you. He hates you. I love you."

"Enough, Klaus. Aie. Aie. Oh that hurts. Hans . . .
please. Do it now."

A squirrel or some other small animal leaped from one
branch of the overhanging beech tree to another. There
was the sound of creaking wood as it landed and then, as if
that were the signal, the grove turned silent. Though I
strained my ears, there was no forest sound to be heard.

Hans squatted on his heels and wiped the necromancer's face with one of our mother's embroidered linen
handkerchiefs.

I thought, "What a tender gesture. Where did he learn it?"

"Persian," my brother said, "I want payment for what I
do. Do you understand?"

"Of course. Anything in my power. But hurry."

"No, no. Haste kills. Tell me, mountebank, how did you get into this fix?"

"Owooo. It hurts."

"Well?"

"It was the saffron vendor, whom you broke."

Hans laughed. "So she told you."

"My beard, Hans. Please. My beard," he gasped. Then, "It was an ill thing you did, Hans. Now, free me from the log."

Hans pulled the Persian's head up roughly by the hair, then let it drop. "Tell me first how she is responsible for this."

The necromancer sighed. "She was a victim. There is no victim so unhappy who cannot be solaced by victimizing someone else. With you gone, the poor young woman needed someone nearby to blame. And I was there.

"She was not far wrong, you know. It was tactless of me to show so blatantly my admiration for your mother. It enraged you and, if the truth be told, it enraged the saffron vendor as well."

"To the point, Persian. How did she put you in this fix?"

"You see," the Persian winced, "when I am not a wise necromancer, I am an ordinary fool. She danced for me.

"After you broke her, she came back to 'me. I bathed her and clothed her in fresh garments. I gave her sleepy potions that helped her to rest. It took two or three weeks of careful tending during which, because she was young, she recovered her health. But all the while that I was looking after her, she was meditating my punishment.

"One sunlit afternoon, she came to my tent and asked me to walk with her in the woods. It seemed a simple enough request. We often strolled in the forest, she to gather herbs and I for the pleasure of her company. I whistled up my cockatoo. With it perched on my shoulder, we started off, but I should have suspected something was wrong when I saw that, for our forest walk, she had chosen to wear her gold-embroidered, pearl-encrusted dancing-girl's dress.

"When we came to this glade, she made me set the cockatoo at the edge of the clearing, then she bade me sit on this log. 'I want to dance for you,' she said. 'I want to make you happy.' I glanced at the log and noticed that it had an iron wedge driven into a cleft down its middle, but I thought no more about it than that some forester had put off until tomorrow work that he had begun today.

"She danced. Prettily enough I suppose, though dancing was never one of her talents. But now there was something wrong with her. She was no longer the young woman I had known. Before you broke her, she used to have a characteristic odor, like honeysuckle. Now, as she danced, the honeysuckle smell was still there, but tainted, as if with the smell of burning sulfur.

"It was late in the day and the sun, as it began to set, enclosed the silver beeches in a rosy glow. I was tired and, like any other desirous old fool, I began to conceive fantasies about how little the difference mattered between my great age and her bright youth. There are old men, you know, who are like leeks—with a white top and a green tail. The cunning woman seemed to know what I was thinking because she danced closer to me and said, 'Close your eyes and I will dance what you dream.'

"I closed my eyes. She whispered, 'Get up on the log, sweet man. There, like that. Crouch down. Keep your eyes closed, and give me your hand. Soon, I will drive you mad. That's it. Now, *feel* me dancing. There. You have the outermost strand of pearls. Smell them. Taste them. There, that's it. Now the second strand, nearer my breast. Bend your head. Bend your head. Feel this caress; and this. And now, the round of my belly as I dance. Feel it. Feel it. Lower. There. That is for your lips. Ah man. Yes, lower. Lower. Ah . . . ah . . . put your tongue to its proper use. There. There. Bend. Easy, now. Slowly. Make the ecstacy last . . . THERE!'

"*Snap*.

"I opened my eyes and saw my saffron vendor standing fully clothed and holding the iron wedge in her hand as I struggled to raise my head, from this.

"How she laughed. Despite all the torment I have had since then, my heart expands when I remember her laughter. 'Let that teach you,' she sang. 'So much for shivering queens.' Her face darkened. 'So much for Hans,' she muttered and flung the iron wedge to the edge of the clearing where it crashed, startling the cockatoo into flight. Then she and the bird fled from the grove, leaving me here."

"Ha! So she remembered me," said Hans. "Good. A pity, though. I should have liked to see her dance."

"That's a horrible story," I complained. "How could you, old man? What about the white light that spills from the sutures of God's skull? What about Microprossopus and Tetragrammaton?"

"Klaus, I've told you. When I am not wise, I am a fool."

"Then the butcher was right," I raged. "Even you. Even . . . she . . . and my mother . . . We are only meat . . . "

"Stop, Klaus. My brain is melting. I'm sweating blood. This is no time for metaphysics. Let your brother free me from the log."

"Meat!" I shouted.

His eyes closed. "Meat," he acquiesced, then, so quietly that I almost did not hear him, "meat and something more." He took a deep breath and called, "Now, Hans. Please. The beard."

Hans climbed onto the log and crouched down until his face was on a level with the Persian's. He ran his fingers over the old man's beard following it from his chin, to the cleft in the log where it disappeared. Then he tugged gently at it.

"Easy, Hans. Easy," the Persian moaned.

"Hmm. Hmm. I see. Hmm." Hans cocked his head in a fair imitation of a physician examining a patient with a difficult illness. He reached into his doublet and removed a clay vial from an inner pocket. With a snap of his fingers, he broke the stopper and, bending so close to the necromancer that I thought he was going to kiss him, he allowed two drops from the vial to run down the beard.

"Nothing to worry about, old man," he said. "Nothing caustic or acerbic. No vitreol, no royal water. Nothing but oil of the catalpa pod. Hold still and let it run down your beard and into the log."

Enviously, I watched my brother. If he hated the world so much, how did he always know what to do? Meanwhile, I was bothered by the lack of noise in the glade. There was no birdsong; no sound of scuttling mice; no hum of bees or the flutter of tiger-butterfly wings. The trees stirred without creaking; my clothes moved without rustling.

We waited. After five minutes, when my brother judged that the oil of catalpa had done its work, he took the Persian's head between his hands and pulled up slowly.

"Stop! It hurts!" The necromancer's eyelids fluttered. Hans paused, then pulled again. "Oh no. I beg you. No."

Hans stopped and wiped drops of foam from the old man's lips. "Listen, Persian," he said. "Half an inch of your beard is no longer in the log. In an hour, all of it will be free. But I can't have you yowling and thrashing about each time I pull your head. Is that clear?"

"Clear, prince. I'll try . . . but oh, Lord how it hurts . . . "

"Now, once more. Hold still while I pull."

"Mmmpfffff."

"And again."

"Mmmmpfffffff."

And so it went. In increments of half an inch at a time. Slowly, the distance between the Persian's chin and the log widened. Sometimes, when the pain was too great, tears spurted from the necromancer's eyes.

An hour later, Hans lifted the Persian's head free of the log. For a moment, the old man continued to crouch on the log, then he passed his hand over his chin. Overwhelmed by the discovery that he was free, he rolled off the log and lay panting in a clump of weeds. I knelt beside him and offered him wine from my pocket flask. He drank greedily.

"Are you rested, necromancer?" Hans asked.

"Yes," he said, still breathing hard. "Ah, Hans. How can I thank you? You've been so kind."

"Never kind. You will remember, I expect to be paid."

The Persian got shakily to his feet. "Of course. Anything at all. But . . . " He must have been feeling better because there was now a sly look in his eyes. "But, Hans. I am a poor man. And an unlucky one. I have lost my ape and my bird. My saffron vendor has gone away. . . . Surely your charity . . . "

"Enough. You know very well what I want."

Hans's pallor was alarming. Then, with a sinking feeling, I understood what he had in mind even as I prayed that I was wrong.

The Persian, who was now as pale as Hans, whined, "How can I know anything? I've lost my saffron vendor, my ape and my bird and have proved myself a fool in the process. You insist on being paid? Very well then, take these. They are the last two coppers I still have in my rags." He held his arm out and showed two coins in the palm of his hand.

"I don't need your stinking coins. I want you to prophesy!"

"Ha, ha, ha," the old man cackled. "Not me. Oh, no. I've given up that trade."

"Persian! I freed you from the log."

"For which, young prince, I will be eternally grateful, but what you ask . . . No. Oh, no. I've lost the knack."

"Did you ever have it, old man? Or were you as much a fraud then as you are now? It's true, isn't it? He grabbed at the Persian's tunic and pulled him forward. "All the cards are blank, aren't they?" he snarled.

The Persian waved his arms weakly. "As God is my witness, I don't know." Hans thrust him away, but continued holding his tunic.

"Well, we'll soon find out. Klaus!"

"I'm going away," I said. "I'm going to find my horse and go away."

"No you won't. You're going to stay here and let our Persian friend find you some clues, some hints and signs. Come on, old man. Here's my fat brother Klaus. Truly a man without destiny. Go on now. You know the old tune: 'The future is a mystery but Tetragrammaton condescends to send you clues.'"

The Persian grimaced. "You remember it, don't you?"

"Of course I do. Come on, now. You practiced your filthy tricks on me. Let's see what you'll show Klaus. Out with your cards."

"I have no bird, Hans. My ape is . . ."

"Damn it, Persian. The boy loves you. Show him his spark."

"Oh yes," I pleaded. "I do. I do love you. Why shouldn't I have a clue?"

"Because the tickets are blank," Hans said. "That's why."

"Are they, Persian?" I asked, putting my hand on his shoulder.

The Persian looked from me to Hans and back at me. "Put my beard back into the log," he said.

"Please, old man," I urged. "Read your tickets for me."

"No."

Hans felled him with his fist. I watched the flower of blood that sprouted on the old man's cheek. "Read your tickets," commanded Hans.

The necromancer coughed and pulled himself erect. Between dry gulps he mumbled, but he was already fumbling in his rags. At last, somewhere in the labyrinth inside them, he found the lacquer box in which he kept his tickets. "Hans," he tried once more, "I have no bird, no cage. How can I prophesy?"

"Just close your eyes, shuffle your cards, and give the top one to Klaus."

I started to tremble. There was Amalasuntha off there on the mile-high glass mountain. Already that day it had occurred to me that my chance to get Amalasuntha was as good as anyone's. No, Hans was wrong. I was not a man without a destiny, or such a thought could not have occurred to me. I gazed into the old man's eyes. They were kind, compassionate. He knew I loved him. He would not be cruel to me.

The Persian shuffled his deck. Then he cried, "No. You were right, Hans. I am a liar. A trickster. A cheat. The cards are all blank."

Icily, Hans said, "Give Klaus his card."

I took the card and turned it over and stared down at it for a long time.

"Well, Klaus, what's the matter? Is it in a language you cannot understand, or have you forgotten how to read?"

"No," I said, my lips parched.

"Well?"

"It says,

> "In the capital of failure
> Failure fails,
> Ride to discover
> What that entails."

I hesitated, then showed my brother the card. The Persian wiped the blood from his cheek. "Persian," Hans was trembling. "Give him another card." The necromancer held out his cards. I took a second one. "Read it, Klaus."

I closed my eyes and bit my lip. "No. I don't want to look."

Hans reached over and pressed the point of his dagger against my neck. "Read it."

I looked down. I read,

> "In the capital of failure
> Failure fails,
> Ride to discover
> What that entails."

"Old man," Hans said, his voice muted, "Do they all say the same thing?"

"Prince, as God is my witness, I don't know."

"Very well then," Hans said. "Shuffle your deck. I'll choose my own card." He looked leached and—withered.

"You want this, prince? It is your express desire? You urge it?"

"Yes." He stood like a statue that has been marred by fire. The Persian shuffled his deck, then held it out to Hans who took one at random and looked down. "No, Persian. There must be a mistake because this card is blank. Give me another."

"Yes, prince." The Persian stood very erect and held out his deck.

Hans chose a second card and looked down. His voice cracked as he said, "It . . . it, too is blank. Give me another."

"Prince," the old man said, "There are twenty-two cards in the deck. Shall I give them all to you?"

"Are they all blank?"

"Hans, as God is my witness, I don't know."

Hans turned and walked stiffly to his horse and mounted. I hurried to the Persian, whose bloody cheek I wiped with a moistened corner of one of my mother's handkerchiefs. When I was done, he gave me a cursory kiss and, whispering "Goodbye," he hurried after Hans who seemed to be waiting for him.

"Hans," the old man said, as if he were begging pardon, "I am only a stumbler, a fool."

"You are neither the one nor the other. I should have killed you long ago. Goodbye." He spat and trotted out of the clearing.

The minute he was gone there was a sound like a pistol shot as a woodpecker attacked a grub in the bark of the beech tree to which his horse had been tethered. That noise was followed by the clear note of a cricket and then a robin's song until finally the wood became a happy jangle of its own music.

Dazed by what I had seen and heard, I might have stood there well into the night had the Persian not brought my white mare to me. "Go, Klaus. Go to your brother."

"No. Let me stay with you? Teach me . . . "

He helped me onto my white mare then slapped her side so hard that she took off at a canter. "Ride, Klaus," he called after me. "To the capital of failure."

Ahead of me, my brother, who had the habit of success, was galloping toward the glass mountain. I had a twinge of pity for my poor horse, who had to bear my massive weight; then I leaned forward and touched her with my spurs.

XXVIII

I HEARD a noise like the chattering of a monkey. It was the harelipped Fritz, jumping up and down in his alcove and shouting, "Miserable bastard. Fat man. How can you sit there indifferent to the most affecting part of my story?"

"Control yourself," I soothed. "The fact is, I've heard you. Every word." Indeed, I had, with that part of my mind that was not engrossed in my own memories of the last time my slender brother and I encountered the Persian necromancer.

"You have?" he said warily. "You paid attention to what I've been saying."

"I heard it," I replied. "You were telling me about your brother Baldur and the miller's daughter. About yourself and the pea-pod and the mill-pond."

"What else?" he asked greedily. "Tell me what else."

"You said," I began, "that once you crossed the pass that led to Amalasuntha's kingdom, you served your brother as an errand boy once more. And, remembering the Persian's verses, you scoured the hamlets and villages on the mountain slope until you found a miller who had a daughter that would suit your brother's needs."

"Ah," Fritz said. "Maybe I've been unkind to you. But . . . but did you hear the part about how Baldur cheated? How he listened to the riddle the Persian gave me to solve? How he violated the law of omens?"

"Yes, but that was long ago, at nearly the very beginning of your story. What you've told me just now is the tale of Baldur's seduction of the miller's daughter."

"Do you remember the verses?" Fritz demanded.

"Of course," I said. "Listen:

> Send the miller's daughter
> To the moonlit mill.
> Let her stand near water
> That flows beneath the wheel.
>
> Give the maiden fever,
> Let her find out signs.
> Touch her like a lover
> But do not touch her loins."

Fritz beamed. "Yes. What a precise mind you have. Go on, please. Tell me the rest of what I said."

"You want me to repeat your story word by word?"

"No, just the part about the miller's daughter."

Despite the hours we had been together in the tower room, I did not feel that I was required to oblige him. Especially since it was clear that he meant to steal the story of my life and annex it to his. I had no intention of gratifying his greedy curiosity. And yet, I gave in to his suggestion. Not, as I'm sure he imagined, out of any sense of identification with him but because it seemed to me that if I retold his story the way he had spoken it, I would ease a little my own burden of loneliness.

"What you said," I began, "was that once again you served as your brother's errand boy."

"No, no," Fritz complained. "You're not *telling* me what I said. You're just dutifully repeating it by rote. Come now, words are not merely air that any voice can imitate. Make me feel that you understood what I said with something more than your ears. Come now," he coaxed gently. "Try again. What did I say?"

"Very well," I said. "Listen. Here, word for word, and nuance by nuance, is what you said:

"It was clear from the Persian's verses that my first task was to find a miller who had a daughter living at home. That turned out to be much easier than I expected. I could hardly ride a mile in any direction without coming to a mill beside a racing brook and every mill was inhabited by a surly miller who had a marriageable beautiful daughter.

"The miller into whose home Baldur and I finally moved was a singularly dirty fellow. A man so brutal and ugly that it took a strenuous act of faith to believe that he was the father of the fresh-faced, hazel-eyed beauty who lived with him.

"She was fifteen years old, an alert, lively young woman who was still child enough to be startled and pleased each morning to discover, when she woke, that she was alive. Graceful, slender, eager and hopelessly innocent, she was the perfect target for Baldur's scheme.

"It was a sorry household in which the squint-eyed miller and I waited for Baldur to accomplish the seduction of the maiden. We sat drinking his sour wine in the dark, timbered room below the loft in which Baldur lay and to which, daily, she came for her arcane instruction. I did not want to hear what took place in the loft between her and Baldur. The miller, on the other hand, eager to hear something lascivious, relished each day's session.

"Baldur did not vary his routine. Always, there was ten minutes of honeyed talk: 'Ah, my love. How beautiful you are. How sensitive. You are the fairest flower of the field. Your lips are scarlet petals, your eyes, bright diamonds, your teeth the purest pearls.'

"She was fifteen years old. He was a prince, handsome and tall who had come riding on a black war horse from a country far away. She listened. She believed. For her reward, Baldur touched her, kissed her, turned her this way, now that. She arched her body in the direction of pleasures her dreams and his fingers hinted at but which he did not allow her to achieve. 'Ah, ah . . . ' she begged. 'And, 'I want . . . oh, how I want . . . ' he replied. Each day, he gave her the illusion that she was about to experience the mystery, and every day his kisses and his caresses stopped at a line below her waist and above her loins.

"The strain on her began to tell. Her eyes sank in her head. She stumbled and shuffled like a village girl hiding a pregnancy. Her skin turned sallow, her hands grew gaunt and dry. Her body shrank until her clothes hung from her frame like the borrowed rags of a scarecrow. Day followed day, and still she climbed the ladder to his loft, determined to learn precisely what he would not teach her.

"Sometimes, when he wanted a respite, he sent her away and she crept down from his loft and dragged herself outside. It was on one such day that I followed her, afraid that she might do herself some harm. I watched as she leaned against a rock beside the mill-race and stared into the clear water at the lower end of the pool. When I saw tears welling in her eyes, I came close and patted her on the shoulder. 'There, there,' I said. 'There, there. I know how you feel.'

'Ah, Fritz, how could you?' Her formerly clear, golden skin had taken on a mealy look; her hazel eyes were bloodshot.

"For a while, I did not answer. Hers was the unhappiness of love, while I was merely lonely. How could I say anything to comfort her? Still, I tried. 'Tell me,' I began, "Can you whistle?'

" 'Of course I can.'

" 'I can't,' I said.

"Her hand flew to her mouth and she gasped. 'Oh, Fritz. I'm sorry.' She tried to look into my eyes, but the sight of my upper lip unsettled her. Hiding her face in her hands she cried, 'Oh, go away. Go away. I need all my pity for myself.'

"Twisting an empty pea-pod between my fingers, I turned and made my way upstream along the trail that went along the mill-race. There, I sat on a stone and watched the water foam against the wheel. It was a fresh, bright afternoon, very cold for spring. The stone I sat on was rough and pitted. Rain had formed tiny pools in its surface, and near one of these the nymph of a dragonfly lay heaving its body, twisting and turning its way over grains of sand, seeking the water which it had lost. Later on, if it lived, it would be a gorgeous red-and-blue-winged creature; now it was a tormented worm. As I brushed it gently back into a water-filled crevice I felt a touch on my shoulder. It was the miller's daughter.

" 'Don't turn around,' she said. 'Just listen.'

" 'I'm sorry, Fritz. I was cruel. I couldn't help it. I know you didn't want to hurt me either.' I kept my eyes on the water and said nothing. 'Look down, Fritz,' she continued.

'Do you see the two stones at the farther end of the pond? There, where the water narrows. Do you see how they form a kind of sluice?' I nodded. 'When I was younger, I used to lie on the smaller flat stone watching the tumbling water. My pleasure was in the spray, the roar and hiss, the cold breath of the water. When droplets stung my face, I laughed.

" 'Then one day, a year ago, on a day as bright as this, I went there. I was going to lie on my rock and let the sun warm me and the water cool my face. When I got here, just where we're standing now, I saw that there was a soldier lying on my rock, belly down, face close to the water. He was young and lean.

" 'For a moment, I thought he was having my kind of pleasure in the interplay of sunlight, warmth and chill. I was so pleased to see him loving it the way I did that I fell in love with him.

" 'In love the way a fourteen-year-old can be in love: intensely, perfectly. I imagined that he would look up and see me; that he would beckon; and that I would run to lie beside him on the other rock; and that we would pass our lives like that, staring at each other across rushing water with the sun beating down and the spring breeze in our hair.

" 'The soldier had nothing like that in mind. He had a shiny kitchen fork held high in his right hand as he watched the water. Suddenly, he moved. I saw a silver glint in the air, heard a splash and his cry, "Got him!" Then he rolled over onto his back and exulted in the trout he had speared. He held the fish out at arm's length to let the sun's rays glisten on it. On its stabbed belly, two bright red drops of blood gathered. The trout wriggled and twisted, head to tail, tail to head, and in the soldier's body there was an answering lust. They were the spearer and the speared.

"'Oh, Fritz. How can you understand my surprise at what I was feeling. You'll say I was outraged at seeing my rock spoiled by his greed. That I hated him for bloodying the place of my pleasure. But it wasn't like that at all. The sunlight on the fish's belly and the drops of blood filled me with joy. And I, watching, felt my body swell and grow packed. If the soldier had called to me I would have run to him without a moment's hesitation.

"'No, Fritz. I turn and twist. I stretch. I blush under my smock. I swell and burn and wait. What does Baldur want? I'm not a child, Fritz. I'm ready. Baldur's fingers half-teach me what I almost know. He touches me here and here but never--here. When I protest, he condescends to me. "Patience dear," he says. "I can't help the way things are. There's destiny in this. We are serving a higher principle. Wait a little longer."

"'Fritz, I'm dying. His caresses are killing me. "Wait," he says. "Wait." Then he says, "When the moon is full, darling. Ours is the mystery of first love for which the light of the full moon is auspicious. Wait darling. Not yet." Then he touches me and sends me away, my blood pounding.'

"'I know. I understand.'

"She talked past me. 'If he loved me, wouldn't he take me in his arms? Wouldn't he make me his own? Ah, I could see dying for him then. To die for a man who loves you makes sense, but to die barren and dry for the sake of a *higher principle*? No, Fritz. It cannot be nice to die for a principle.'

"I looked straight before me, then I reached back and took her hand. The mill-race roared. She said, 'In three days the moon will be full. What will happen then, do you think? Will he keep his promise, or is he doing this because he enjoys tormenting me?'

"I turned around and brushed the tips of her fingers with an unruined corner of my upper lip and said, 'You are beautiful. If it were me, I wouldn't wait.'

"I felt her stiffen. 'Don't,' she said. 'You'll only make us miserable.' When I caressed her hand, she spoke harshly, 'Don't do that. Don't you see . . . Oh, Fritz. It's not my fault. I can't help the way things are.'

"I loved her. Just the same I said what I knew would hurt her. 'Isn't that what Baldur says?' She tore her hand away from me and fled.

"I sat where I was and watched the two flat rocks in the middle of the stream and thought of the soldier and his trout. From time to time, I tried to kiss the cool pea-pod I had been carrying but my lips were not made for kissing and I flung it away.

"Three nights later, the moon was full. The miller and I sat in his untidy room drinking his sour red wine and watched his daughter crawl up the ladder to Baldur's loft. The miller, already drunk, winked at me and said, 'Ho, now it begins.'

"I stared into my glass and saw nothing I had not seen before. In the loft, there was the sound of a scuffle as Baldur commenced his love-making. I heard her body roll and bump as he turned her, twisted her, touched her. I heard her heels drum on the floor and her swift, choked breathing. Then silence followed by a muffled weeping.

"In the eaves, there was a flutter of wings and a scolding *chk, chkchk* from the orioles nesting there. The miller's daughter sniffled. I assume she sat up because I heard her delighted cry, 'Baldur, look. Moonlight. The moon is full. Look. Is it now, Baldur? Now?'

"I heard Baldur's voice but what he said was not clear. He talked for a very long time, evidently giving her instructions because she replied, 'No, I'm scared.'

'Now,' he said. 'This is the night. Go, now.'

"I heard her dragging step, then I watched as she backed down the ladder, looking old and sick. I followed her outside and watched her painful passage along the side of the mill. She went like a blind woman, tapping at the timbers with numb fingers. When she reached the corner of the mill below the rafters in which the orioles had their nest, she leaned against an elm tree and looked up toward the birds. I, enclosed in shadows, sat on the rock where the dragonfly nymph had lost its way, and watched.

"In the bright moonlight, I could see the blank look in her eyes. Worn and cold and sick, she cowered against the tree while the trout in the pond behind her touched blunt noses or leaped into the air and fell back into the water. A frog, one of whose legs had been sheared off by the mill-wheel, leaned crookedly on a rock and stared down at its blood forming a thread down the side of the stone and into the water.

"The orioles chirped. An old bear in the woods across from the mill-race snuffled for honey in a hollow tree; a doe sneezed; a clapper rail said something to the night, its complaint like a file across a nerve. I passed my tongue across my lower lip.

"She waited. An hour after the frog had slipped from its white stone and was carried belly upward over the rim of the mill-pond, she heard the orioles.

"Startled, she looked around to see if the voice came from someone nearby. Then, amazed, she understood that what she heard were the birds. *Twit, twit, twit, twit, twit, twit, twitter, twit*.

"The hen replied, *Twitter, twit, twit, twit, twit, twit*.

"Both birds said petulantly, *Chk, chkchkchkchk, chk, chk*.

"There was a fluttering in the nest and then the hen said, *Twitter twit*, 'what have you got?'

"*Twitter, twitter*, 'goat's hair,' answered the cock.

" 'What are you waiting for? Give it here.'

" 'Who else is it for?'

" 'That's not enough. Get more.'

" 'You go,' said the cock. 'I'm tired.'

" 'Where did you get it?'

" 'A billy goat at the Fox.'

" 'What does that mean, a billy goat at the fox?'

" 'It means that there's an inn due east of here called the Sign of the Fox. And the inn has a courtyard in which there's a billy goat. The goat has hair. And the hair you have is from his tail.'

" 'At the inn due east of here,' said the hen, 'at the Sign of the Fox where there's a billy *twitter, twit, twitter, twit, twit, twit*. All right, you sit, I'll fly.' And she was off, making a brief streak of shadow in the moonlight.

"The miller's daughter drooped and would have fallen but I caught her and led her back to the mill, past her father who lay snoring with his head twisted to one side on his rough-hewn oak table. I set her feet on the ladder. I helped her climb toward Baldur. Then I took my place beside the miller and hoped that his snores would drown out whatever was about to happen in the loft.

"This time, it was her voice I heard as she reported what she had heard to Baldur. When she was done, she asked prettily, 'Will you love me now?'

"There was a *thwack* as he kicked her into a corner. I heard the sliding sound of her skirt as she crawled back to him. 'Now?' she said. Baldur had a well-shaped foot. His next kick sent her back the entire distance she had crawled. When she pulled herself back a second time, she whispered, 'Love me. Now.'

'No,' he said, 'not now. Not ever.'

"She was young and strong. 'I waited,' she said. 'I heard the birds. You said . . . '

"The sound of his kick was precise and clean. I knew what he was doing in the silence that followed. He was smoothing his waistband. When he was done, he said, 'You know. Not everyone gets a chance to be useful in this world. Count yourself lucky. Farewell.'

"He came down from the loft in a whirl of energy. 'Up Fritz. It's time to ride.'

"I shook off my night lethargy and bent to my boots. A beam of early sunlight struck the sleeping miller's eyelid. He puckered his nose. 'Well,' Baldur said from the threshold where he waited for me. 'Get moving.' Though my shoulders ached, I got moving.

"I had, first, to climb into the loft to get Baldur's spurs and riding crop. When I got there, the miller's daughter was just dropping into the noose she had made from one of Baldur's shirts. I cut her down and knelt beside her while I rubbed warmth back into her body. Her beautiful lips were parted, her clothing askew. It was my chance to kiss her, to touch her breasts. Instead, I chafed her wrists and begged her to wake up.

"At last she opened her eyes and said, 'Ah, Fritz. Why did you cut me down?'

" 'Because you must live. You are young and strong and beautiful.'

" 'I've lived too long. What's to become of me? No, no, no. Put me back in the noose.'

"I lifted her head and eased my lips into her hair. 'Hush. Hush and let me tell you about owls.'

"Her eyes widened. 'You're mad, Fritz. You must be mad. I want to hang myself and you try to distract me with stories about owls.'

" 'Not distract. No. But yes. I know about owls. Listen. You know there are many kinds of owls in the world.

" 'All those owls eat. One barn-owl in a single year eats two hundred and nineteen thousand locusts, eight hundred mice and eighty small birds. In the barn-owl's crop, they are certainly dead. But before that each one of those locusts, every one of the mice and all the small birds lived long enough to have memories before they died. As the barn-owl did before it was killed by a hawk; and as the hawk did before the hunter . . . "

" 'Oh stop, Fritz.' She smiled wanly. 'Stop. You have no talent for preaching to a broken heart.'

'No talent. No doubt. But listen . . . ' And here I felt my heart beating wildly. 'I'm going to ride for Amala . . . that is, Baldur and I are about to ride . . . But . . . But . . . I know what a poor sort of thing I am . . . hardly a match for a beautiful young woman . . . still . . . I am a . . . prince. And though I can't whistle . . . or kiss . . . I can . . . I . . . Well there are other ways . . . What I'm trying to say is that . . . if you could see your way . . . if you would . . . '

"She looked up into my face, then turned her head aside. 'Oh Fritz . . . poor, dear Fritz. Don't.'

" 'You could, you know,' I hurried on. 'You might, if you put your mind to it . . . you might even learn to kiss . . . you know . . . One can kiss with one's eyes closed. And not all kissing has to be done with lips.' My lips were in her hair. My hands gripped her shoulders. 'You could, you know. Even if only once, even under compulsion. Even if you held your breath. Who knows what might happen then . . . '

"She shuddered. 'Stop!' she begged. 'No, no, no, no.'

"I wound a ringlet of her hair around my finger and put my cheek to it. 'Yes,' I said. 'I see what you mean.' Then I took Baldur's spurs and his riding crop and backed down the ladder. From the threshold of the miller's filthy room I called back, trying to keep my voice steady so it would be heard over the miller's snores. 'Goodbye.'

"From the loft where I was sure she was either pressing Baldur's pillow to her breast or else retying his shirt into a noose, I heard her hollow, 'Goodbye, Fritz.' Then nothing more. I waited another moment, hoping for who knows what, but there was nothing more to hear except the miller's snores. A minute later, I clattered after Baldur up the rock-strewn path that led from the mill to the road. Somewhere due east of us there was an inn called The Sign of the Fox."

XXIX

"IT'S astonishing," Fritz the harelip said. "Amazing! You actually remember every word I said. I would have sworn you heard nothing, but now it appears you've treasured my least syllable."

"Remembered," I corrected.

"Even so, my story suits you. You tell it as if it were your own. You've no idea how beautiful it makes you look."

"Fat men aren't beautiful.'

"Ah, but you are. My words on your tongue create just that warping of focus that makes you beautiful and our story poignant."

"Will you let me get on with it?"

"Certainly." He was entranced.

"I hate being interrupted."

He smiled one of those gaping smiles of his. At the sight of it, my mouth ached and I put my hand to my upper lip to still the pulsing there. I felt uneasy telling his story. It was as if by telling it, I was getting to know him too well.

"I promise," he said. "I won't interrupt again."

"You'll have to remind me. Where was I?"

"You were saying, 'It was well past dawn when we turned from the mill and rode off to find . . .'"

"That's enough. If I'm to tell your story, be still and let me tell it."

"Of course."

In my own fat man's voice, and with my own emphasis, I resumed the retelling of the harelip's story which went like this:

"It was well past dawn when we turned from the mill and rode off to find the goat the orioles had talked of. The taste of last night's bad wine was a scum in my mouth. The long hillside down which we rode was covered with pines. The odors of the morning—crushed pine needles, the smoke of wood fires, the smell of broken mushrooms and trodden fern—rose with the morning mist. In the dense stands of trees through which we rode, the bluejays called to each other. A flock of Lapland swans, trying to make their way north past the pellucid space that was Amalasuntha's mountain, made erratic circles just beneath a bank of fluffy white clouds. There was a chill in the air which, through my gloves, felt colder than it was.

"We were two princes riding on a bright spring morning. Baldur rode with an air of abstraction while I sat slumped in my saddle grieving for the miller's daughter, and, if the truth be told, for myself. I was sick of the way my brother always had his way. I resented his good looks and his skill, and I hated myself for doing his bidding.

"The Sign of the Fox was a wretched country inn halfway down the mountainside where the barbarian goatherders stopped to rest their flocks on their way to and from the spring grass. The inn, not much more than a ramshackle shed, stood in the center of a boggy courtyard on one side of which there was a pen in which there bleated and jostled three hundred nanny goats. A crowd of goat-herds, who were eating and drinking at low tables on a porch before the inn, watched us curiously as we rode through the fallen gates.

"The nanny goats in their pen cowered, making a terrible din. '*Meh, meh, meh!* they cried and pressed against each other as they stretched their necks to the sky in the painful way such creatures have when they are frightened or lustful. They might have been both because, not twenty yards away, in a smaller pen, there stood the billy goat about which the orioles had talked.

"He was enormous. A stinking beast who stood four feet high in the shoulders. A king goat; an emperor goat, with a head as large as a tall man's shield. His yellow eyes blazing, he stood trembling astride his own great ballocks. Each of his legs was tied with a stout rope to a different oak sapling. From the strain on the ropes, there was every reason to believe that there was imminent danger that the creature would break loose.

"As we rode in, the innkeeper, who had just finished retying one of the ropes, looked up. Wiping his hands on his apron, he came toward us. 'A sad day, gentlemen,' he said, by way of greeting. 'A sad day. Cheating and corruption on every hand. See! Thirty years as an innkeeper and this is what gets foisted on me instead of the king's good coin. Tell me, what am I to do with this beast?'

"The terrible smell of the goat made Baldur's stallion nervous. He pranced in place; he backed and bucked. Baldur quieted him and studied the goat. 'Why does it tremble like that?'

"The innkeeper sad, 'It's blind and randy.'

" 'What?'

" 'Yes, prince. The damn beast was left by a softly smiling Persian who spent a few days here. Him and his pretty apprentice. Who would have taken such a gentle fellow to be one of the world's worst rogues? Now he's gone, and his saucy lady, too, leaving me with that . . . ' he spat in the direction of the goat.

" 'Why is he blind?' I asked.

" 'A Persian custom, prince. This is a fighting goat, raised for the arena. A blood sport in that barbarian country. They blind the creatures at birth, then keep them penned in for five years. After that, they turn a couple of the beasts loose in the arena.' He licked his lips. 'And to see the two of them. Such gentle folk. So kind. So well-spoken. Well, what's done is done. It's what comes of having a trusting heart.'

" 'Will you sell him to me, innkeeper?' Baldur asked.

" 'What?'

" 'Yes. Sell him. How much do you want for him?'

" 'A blind goat, prince. A virgin blind goat, raised for the arena. A fierce goat. A champion. Oh, he's easily worth his weight in gold.'

" 'In Persia, maybe,' Baldur said. 'What's he worth here?'

" 'Hm, hm. A powerful goat. There isn't his like in the country.'

" 'Well?'

" 'Ah, prince. That takes thinking on. Why don't you make me an offer?'

" 'How much was the Persian's bill?'

" 'The bill? Oh yes, the bill. Well, for the two of them, what with lodging and meat and drink, and fodder for the goat, of course, it was . . . ' He scratched his head, counted on his finger, looked inside his shirt, looked toward the goat-herds who were watching the transaction from the porch. 'It was . . .yes, exactly two hundred and forty-six thalers, pounds, sovereigns, rials and rupiyahs.'

" 'That much?'

" 'Yes. Two hundred and—how much did I say . . . yes, two hundred and forty-six . . . '

" 'Very well,' said Baldur. 'I'll take him.'

"The innkeeper looked aggrieved. 'Come, prince. Is that princely behavior. To close at the first number offered? I am a poor man. I must live. Let us put our heads together.'

"Baldur turned his horse's head. "Come on Fritz, let's go. The poor man has dreams of dancing ducats. Goodbye, innkeeper.'

"I touched my heels to my mare's side. She turned, more than willing to leave that dangerous courtyard, but I knew better than to think we would go very far.

" 'On the other hand,' the innkeeper called after us, 'an offer is an offer and not to be refused out of hand. Let's discuss the matter, prince. Perhaps you will dismount and take some wine?'

" 'No wine, innkeeper. I've agreed to your price. Let me have the goat.'

" 'Slowly, prince. Patience rides a quicker steed than haste. Suppose I do sell you the goat at the price named? He is a fierce creature. Dangerous. How can I be sure you can handle him? If he gets loose, there'll be the devil to pay. There may be damage to my inn. Goat-herds hurt. Nanny goats ravished. Think, prince. Where's equity?'

"Baldur looked from the goat to the innkeeper. "All right. Out with it. What do you want?'

" 'A premium. A small premium. Pay the Persian's bill, and throw in your horse. For equity's sake. It's only just.'

"Baldur dismounted, flung the reins of his stallion to me and started toward the goat, picking his way so cleverly through the mire that there was hardly a trace of mud on his boots.

"The innkeeper splashed after him calling, 'Prince. Oh prince.'

"Baldur paused beside one of the ropes that held the goat. 'Well?' he asked.

" 'The money, prince. What else?'

"Baldur untied his purse and counted out the requisite number of coins, then turned again to the goat.

" 'Prince,' whined the innkeeper. 'You are forgetting.'

" 'What now?'

" 'Your stallion, sire. Your brother holds his reins as if he meant to keep him.'

"It was true. The minute I caught Baldur's bridle I was fired with the hope that his stallion would be mine. Baldur had after all, stolen my riddle. The easier riddle the kindly Persian had given me:

> If, once upon a time, the king of an island kingdom that is famous for its horses should, on a Sunday, say of a stallion in the third stall from the left in his stable that it was a goat weighing six hundred pounds and that it was twelve years old with a long beard and glaring yellow eyes, and that it needed a nanny to mount, how would it smell?

"Slow thinker that I was, I had, just the same, figured out that no matter what the king said of his stallion, it would still smell like a horse. So that, on the face of it, I had solved my riddle. But Baldur, cheat that he was, though he had been warned not to, had listened to the riddle and, being subtle as a serpent, had instantly divined a deeper meaning. And now he was about to reap the reward of his skill. It was only fair, then, that I should have something for myself.

"Impatiently, Baldur called,'Give him the horse, Fritz.' I heard him, but did nothing. The innkeeper sloshed his way back to me and, unbending my fingers from Baldur's bridle, took the stallion from me.

"Baldur, standing beside the trembling goat, called, 'Somebody! Get me an axe.'

"I dismounted from my mare and walked toward the porch where the goat-herds sat watching us. 'An axe,' I called. "Does one of you have an axe?' But, whether it was the sight of my ruined face or whether it was that they could not understand what I was saying, they stared mutely at me and did not move. Finally, a seven- or eight-year-old boy threw an axe down from an upper window. Fortunately, I caught a glimpse of its glittering blade and was able to catch it in midair.

"As I approached the billy goat's pen, the three hundred nannies, sensing their danger (or desiring it) set up a high-pitched clamor. Baldur beckoned to the innkeeper, who came apprehensively, leading the black stallion.

" 'The horse is mine, prince,' he said. 'Remember.'

" 'The horse, yes, but we've said nothing about the saddle or the bridle.'

"The innkeeper, who could think of no reply, stood with his mouth open while I removed the gear. When I put the saddle on the goat, the creature, though he accepted it, stiffened, but he absolutely refused the bit, writhing his head and twisting it away from me. Finally, I made a spring of my middle finger and thumb and snapped a sharp fillip to his nose. Startled, he opened his mouth to bleat and in that instant I placed the bit. He clamped his mouth shut, then opened it again, roaring.

"Baldur mounted, tested his stirrups and took the reins in his left hand. He fidgeted, trying to find a comfortable horseman's seat on the trembling goat. The innkeeper retreated to a safe distance. The goat-herds on the inn porch moved their chairs back nearer to the wall. Axe in hand, I stood beside the rope that bound the goat's rear left leg. Bent forward along the goat's arched neck, Baldur had the look of a bent bow.

"He looked around the courtyard as his right hand explored the seams of his tunic, a gesture that struck me as a delaying action. I remember thinking, 'Can it be that Baldur is afraid?'

"Then Baldur shouted, 'Cut' and I brought the axe down on the rope. There was a noise like the clicking of steel teeth. The taut rope, suddenly severed, lashed forward and slapped the goat's flank. 'Beh,' the creature howled and plunged toward the sky tearing the other ropes like so many threads. I jumped back and stumbled against my mare, who reared in panic. I caught her bridle and hung on even as the goat raked her side with a horn as it bucked toward the courtyard gate. I managed to get into my saddle, then I was off, following Baldur on his goat. Behind me, I heard the grief of three hundred nanny goats rising in tremolo toward the sky."

XXX

"BALDUR, ahead of me, was not so very jaunty to look at just then. Perched on his blind, big ballocked animal, he looked like a wobbling monkey. Over him and his goat there hovered a cloud of stink. Nevertheless. years of elegant horsemanship stood him in good stead so that he retained the look of a cavalier as he kept his goat in a semblance of control.

"We rounded a turn and came out into open country. Here, there were more cottages with smoke rising from their chimneys. The sprouting barley stood stiffly to attention while crows did such damage in the fields as they could. On our right, a brook which, in the summer, would be a thin trickle was now a rushing torrent. Below us, on the plain, we could see the long line of young men who were riding, like ourselves to the other end of the valley where there rose Amalasuntha's glass mountain.

"Riding behind Baldur, I had a clear view of what happened next. Twenty yards in front of him a rabbit broke from a field to our right and started across his path. The sudden blur of white it made darting into the road frightened my mare. She reared and whinnied, but gentle pressure from my knees and on her reins brought her to her senses, but the rabbit, terrified by the tall shadow my rearing mare had made, froze in the middle of the road and cowered there, trying to shrink into itself.

"Because Baldur's face was set and his eyes were glazed, I can't actually say that he saw the rabbit. What is clear is that he made no move to change the goat's direction. The rabbit trembled, but waited patiently as the blind beast lunged toward it, bleating. The goat raised its great head toward the sky and leaped and its right fore hoof, like a dainty piston, made a downward stroke that broke the rabbit's neck and left a dirty imprint on what had been spotless fur. The unexpected touch of his hoof against soft flesh threw the goat into contortions. It shook its head, sending ropes of black saliva flying. 'Behhhhhh' it cried and rolled its blind yellow eyes as it fought the weight on its back and the petrified sexuality it carried between its legs.

"Baldur maintained his riding school seat. When the goat's frenzy subsided, with his free hand, Baldur drew a gold-colored silk handkerchief from a breast pocket and wiped his forehead and the palms of his hands after which he folded and replaced it as he looked around like a man trying to readjust a disordered landscape. He passed his tongue across his lips, then his face resumed its habitual look of calm indifference. Behind us, flies were already gathering over the rabbit's blood-soaked corpse.

"When we reached the long straight road in the valley that led like an arrow straight to the glass mountain, the morning was far advanced. The air was mild, softened by the sun's ascent and yet, despite the occasional farmer in a roadside field, the countryside felt empty. The people had gone to watch the princes making their daily futile assault against the glass.

"Though Baldur was in full control of his goat, the beast continued to tremble, and now, my mare, made uneasy by the hundreds of horses ahead of us on the Line of Approach, also showed signs of restlessness, shying at the slightest noise. When I chastised her she coughed and snuffled. Her breathing became rough, as if she were trying to loosen a grain of barley from her nostrils or from somewhere deep in her throat.

"Exasperated, I yanked at her bit and almost said, 'Stop it. Don't you know that today is my wedding day?' It was an absurd notion, but I clung to it. Why shouldn't this be the happiest day of my life? It was a sunlit day. I was young. And there, ahead of us, the sunlight at the tip of Amalasuntha's mountain created a coronal in whose center it seemed to me that I could see the palanquin in which Amalasuntha sat, waiting for me.

"That golden image faded when my glance fell on Baldur. Had he been mounted on a frog, his graceful air would not have left him. In a while, he would gather in the reins of his goat; he would lean forward in his saddle and then, with a touch of his spurs, he would gallop the last hundred yards of the Line of Approach and charge up the glass where he would achieve what was not even his heart's desire.

"Just then, we found ourselves passing through a rude fair that had sprung up on both sides of the road. It was another of those temporary villages where the princes on the Line of Approach could dismount and while away some time before resuming the ride that had so far proved fatal to all who attempted it. This small fair, like the others, was pervaded by an atmosphere of nervous exhilaration as the young men traded boasts. Some watched fighting cocks or threw darts or dice while others stood around eating and drinking at the various booths that had been set up to serve them. Whatever they did, their real mood was that of soldiers on the eve of a battle that no one expected to win.

"It was here, as we passed a food vendor's stall, that I smelled meat roasting on a charcoal fire and realized suddenly that I was hungry. I called, 'Hey, Baldur. Stop.' For a wonder, Baldur reined in his goat and joined me, but the sound of the meat sizzling on the nearby brazier unnerved the goat. He humped and bucked and would have reared but just then the Persian stepped out from behind the stall and said, 'Hush, Billy.'

The great beast heaved a sigh, put his head down, and closed his eyes. For all intents and purposes, he was asleep.

"Baldur regarded the Persian with distaste. 'So,' he said. 'It's you.'

"'Evidently.' He studied Baldur astride the goat and said, 'I see you've been at your riddle.'

"'I paid you for it. It was mine to solve.'

"'And what about you, Fritz? Have you solved yours?'

"'Yes,' I said.

"The Persian looked into my face so tenderly that I was almost able to forget my fatherless infancy, the long saga of my brother's coldness and my mother's imperfect love. It seemed to me that I could actually feel my upper lip healing. Had I been the old man's child, I would have climbed into his lap where, with a look, I would have implored him, to scold—no, to punish—my imperious brother. 'So, Fritz.' The old man touched my cheek. 'You solved the riddle? You remember. "A king of an island kingdom, horses, stallion, six hundred pounds, glaring eyes, a nanny to mount. How would it smell?"'

"'Like a horse,' I exclaimed and, in the instant, I was seized with such a rancor against my brother that I rushed on heedlessly, "He cheated you know. Baldur, who wasn't supposed to hear my riddle, heard it.'

"'Is that true, prince?' the old man asked, turning to Baldur. 'Did you overhear his riddle?'

"'What if I did?'

"'You surprise me, prince,' the Persian said. 'A man of your intelligence violating the law of omens. And a necromancer into the bargain. Surely you didn't?'

"'Mine was the harder riddle. I did not really cheat. It's you who didn't play fair, telling the easier riddle to my simpleton brother just because he loves you. Since I did not have his advantage, I used my head. In both riddles a choice was obviously to be made between horse and goat. Since "horse" was the solution to Fritz's conundrum, "goat" was clearly the one for mine.'

"'So you used your head,' the Persian said. 'And yet,' he said gravely, 'to violate the law of omens? I don't know. I don't know. Have you no misgivings, prince?'

"'None,' Baldur said, wheeling his goat about. 'Because the truth is, the law of omens is on the side of the strong.'

"'Is that true, old man?' I asked.

"Unperturbed, the Persian replied, 'It's what your brother says.'

"'Then what chance have I got? He'll get Amalasuntha.'

"'That's as may be,' the old man said. 'Now, Fritz, bend down to take my blessing.' I leaned down from my saddle, expecting him to touch my forehead with his lips. Instead he pulled me almost off my mare as he kissed me full on the mouth.

"It was the first time in my life I had ever been kissed that way. Every nerve in my body sang and I turned dizzy even as I heard the old man's voice in my ear, 'You kiss well, Fritz. Take my blessing. Endure a little longer. And ride.'

"To Baldur, he said, 'And you, prince?' he said. 'Will you take my blessing?'

"Baldur bent to adjust his stirrups, 'I've got all I ever needed from you.'

"It was then that the saffron vendor stepped out from behind the booth where the meat was cooking. She carried two skewers of meat on a tray and offered one to Baldur and the other to me. Baldur sniffed at the broiled meat, then he looked closely at the young woman and from her to the old man. 'Hey Persian?' he said. 'Isn't that your sleepy-head?'

" 'See for yourself,' the old man said. I stared and stared. It was, indeed the woman in an opium daze I had found in a brothel. She was as beautiful as when I found her, but now she looked clean and alert in a tidy long-sleeved cotton dress that buttoned to her throat. She looked at the Persian with the fond, proprietary glance of a favorite granddaughter who knows she can do no wrong.

"I loved the serenity with which she moved. Her almond-shaped gray eyes were clear, like those of a child who was wakened from a sweet sleep. When she had given Baldur and me our skewers of meat, she stood beside the Persian and watched us as curiously as we had watched her.

"I remembered the moment in the brothel when she had moved under my touch while all around us the cavern had rustled with the cries of lovers on their shelves. She had put her cheek against my shoulder. She had whispered in my ear and touched me. She would have kissed me, I know, but someone struck a match and even opium could not soften the view of my mouth.

"In that cavern, she had been all dark and warm and limp. A soft creature, unused to wind or sunlight and moved by no other feeling than the lethargic eros that opium created in her blood. Now, as she stood beside the Persian, she looked fit enough to keep up with reapers in a field at planting or at harvest time.

"Baldur, his eyes on her, put the skewer of meat to his mouth and took a bite which he instantly spat out. 'Seared to a crisp, woman,' he growled as he flung meat and skewer aside.

"I tried to say that the meat was good. That it was tender and juicy, but, with by difficult mouth, I managed only to splutter.

" 'What have you done to her, Persian?' Baldur scoffed. 'When I saw her last, she had a certain voluptuous charm. Now she looks as if she's had the fun leached out of her.'

" 'No,' the mountebank said, 'I've wakened her and cleaned her, nothing more.'

"Baldur assumed a confidential air and said, 'Hey, girl, tell the truth. Don't you miss the cavern where by brother found you?'

" 'No, I don't.'

" 'So you've given up the beast with two backs?'

" 'I'm not a beast.'

" 'Amazing. As I recall, you had a sleepy talent that way.'

" 'It's more that I can recall about you.'

"The blood fled from Baldur's cheek. 'Bitch,' he muttered through clenched teeth. 'Come on, Fritz. I have a mountain to ride.' Then he twisted the goat about with a vicious pull at the reins and sent it trotting stiffly, as if it were on stilts, toward the Line of Approach.

"I gave the young woman my empty skewer. 'Thanks,' I said. 'You're welcome,' she said softly, then, her eyes on the receding Baldur, she said, 'A pity, that brother of yours. How skillfully he uses his head. I wonder what he thinks his heart is for.'

"Amazed by what she had said, I started to tell her how my mother, in the form of a turkey buzzard, had, in one of my childhood dreams, opened Baldur's chest with a claw and traded her heart for his. But I did not get to say anything because just then I inadvertently touched my mare's sides with my spurs. She took the bit in her teeth and raced after Baldur whose goat was galloping well past the other riders on the Line of Approach to the glass mountain."

XXXI

"FOR a brief interval, there was a helter-skelter confusion as Baldur and I raced down the final stretch of the Line of Approach. The riders ahead of us, seeing Baldur on his strange mount and hearing the clatter we made, turned aside to watch us pass.

"The goat, exacerbated by blindness and the ache in his huge testicles, reared and pirouetted, fighting the man on his back. Baldur managed to sustain his forward motion by raking the goat's sides with his spurs and beating him about the head with the butt of his riding crop. Suddenly, there was a cheer from the riders closest to the glass mountain. Baldur's goat was on the glass, and climbing.

"As the sound of those voices died, my mare, too, was on the glass.

"She moved with a fine gait, a regular, unstrained trot. Her hooves made a pleasant *tlic, tlic, tlic*, much unlike the pistol shot *clack, clack, clack* of the goat's hooves ahead of me. My muscles moved freely. We were climbing the glass because we liked climbing, and glass was as good a turf as any other. My toes arched and my nerves and my brain expanded with happiness.

" 'It *is* my wedding day,' I thought. 'My horse and I are trotting up the unclimbable mountain. I will have Amala-suntha soon.' My nostrils flared. My fingernails, my teeth, my kneecaps, my eyelashes did as they were told. My lips, in that moment, seemed capable and firm.

"My mare slowed to a walk and ambled up the glass as if she were in a meadow looking for tufts of grass on which to nibble. She set one hoof down after another, the way she would have done on any dusty hillside.

"I looked behind me and saw that we were more than halfway up the mountain. The riders on the Line of Approach looked like dots on a map. I looked ahead and say Baldur's goat leaping and lunging. Baldur had lost his riding-school manner. His hands at the bridle looked like a taxidermist's dream of claws. His face was drawn and his clothing was stained with sweat. His hat hung sideways on his head; his once sleek gauntlets were covered with clots of spume. Though his seat was still good, it no longer looked easy. Still, he and his goat plunged on.

"The wonder was that my mare, moving at a lazy walk, was catching up to the strenuously climbing goat. After ten minutes, we were abreast of him and I could see that Baldur's face was set in a mask of control as he slashed at his animal's sides with his Spanish spurs.

"For one instant, I dreamed neither of us was there. That we were simply two affectionate brothers out on a Sunday ride in their father's woods and meadows; that, fatigued by the summer's heat, we were now looking for a cool brook beside which to dismount where we could drink great draughts of clear cool water and doze for an hour in the shade of a catalpa tree.

"Above us, some luckless bird, flying north, smashed against the glass. The sound shattered my fantasy and I was aware that Baldur's goat was stumbling. I was so close to

Baldur that I could have kissed him. His eyes looked faded, indistinct. I leaned toward him and put my hand out to him, but he waved it away.

" 'Baldur,' I urged, 'Ssssay sssssomething.'

"His shoulders drooped, his face was the color of clay. He continued to ride for another minute but his legs were no longer in their stirrups and he had let his reins drop. He was past wonder, past help. 'Baldur,' I begged. 'Look at me, Baldur.'

"He did, and I looked into the eyes of a slain wolf.

"The goat, in his own agony, drew his body together and climbed the air in a final spasm at whose climax he emitted a thin bleat and fell, thwacking his great ballocks against the glass. Goat and rider formed a splattered statue that tumbled and slid downward past me.

"It was a sun-filled morning. My mare, as if she had always known how to climb glass, moved steadily upward. I sat quietly in the saddle, holding the reins lightly in my left hand. When I leaned forward and patted her neck, her skin quivered as if she were rejecting a fly."

XXXII

HERE, I paused in my retelling of the harelip's story. "Is something wrong?" Fritz asked. "Are the events of my life too much for you?"

"In a way," I could not help admitting. "You sound so very convincing."

"Of course I do," Fritz said. "I have an advantage."

"Oh, what is that?"

"My story is true, fat man."

"So is mine, Fritz."

"How would I know? Have you told me anything?"

His answer made me uneasy. I struggled to find a more comfortable position to accommodate my heavy thighs on his bumpy, animated bed. "I'm sorry," I said. "I can't oblige you. We are much different, you and I. You have genius for uttering yourself. I'm a more inward person. I live inside my head."

"Yes, but whose?" Fritz said.

"Please," I began, "don't push me. The night is almost over and I'll be gone soon. I . . . I've learned to like you. Against my will, if the truth be told. And if it's any comfort to you, I despise your brother. Baldur. So you see, I'm on your side. Please," I all but begged. "Please. Why do you want to force me to be what I'm not?"

"Because there are two of us," he said bitterly. "And we

are here. The map of the flat world is made and we've made it. With the exception of the ten-mile square to the north where Amalasuntha is, we've touched every inch of the world. You know how I got here, because I've kept nothing back. But you, you've guarded your precious silence to the end."

"Silence," I said, "is the beginning of wisdom."

Fritz laughed. "Fatuous nonsense. It is neither the beginning nor the end of anything. It is a negative quality without form or echo. For you, fat man, it is the easiest kind of evasion."

"Yes, maybe you're right," I said, then clamped my mouth shut.

Suddenly, he was enraged. Jumping down from his alcove, he crossed the space between us in two strides and shouted, "Maybe, maybe, maybe. God damn it! If maybe's going to be your game, then get your fat bottom off my bed."

"All right. If that's what you want." I rose and, sidling around him, made my way to his alcove where I sat down. The stone was still warm from his flesh. For a long moment, he stood with his back to me and studied the bed.

When I could bear his silence no longer, I asked, "What are you going to do?"

He did not answer. Then he bent over the bed and pursued with his palm something that rolled back and forth forming lumps first in one place then another. Evidently, he saw something, because, with an impatient jerk, he flung himself on his knees beside the bed, shoved his hands into a rent in the coverlet and grasped at something squirming in the mattress.

Whatever it was resisted him. He yanked and hauled. but despite his enormous strength, he could not pull it loose. "Cursed thing," he said, his voice thick with phlegm. "God forsaken, unnecessary, reptilian, stinking BIRD!" He fell back from the opening in the coverlet. For a moment, I could not see what he had in his hands. Then there was a dry *grrrrrrrrk* and a cockatoo flapped and wriggled out of his grasp. It squawked and fluttered about between us, strutting, preening its moist feathers.

"Hey," I said, "that's the Persian's bird."

"Yes?" he said, "How would I know?" He continued to stare at the bed. "Hey!" he shouted, and plunged his hands back into the hole in the mattress. "What have we here?"

Again there was a prolonged wrestling and a moan that ended on a sort of bleat. Fritz braced himself against the bed and tugged. Slowly his arms came out of the hole. Slowly, slowly, he dragged an enormous goat out by its horns. The animal was more dead than alive. In the corners of its eyes, the maggots were snipping their way out of the eggs their mothers had laid in its flesh. A few of them were already chewing at the corners of its jaws. "Yaaaaaaaaghhhh," Fritz retched and dragged the languid, wet beast to one side of the tower room where it lay, its forelegs bent kangaroo-fashion, its hind quarters frozen in the air like those of a dog whose back has been broken.

The harelip rose to his feet and faced me. "God," he said, "it feels good to clean up. Let's see what else there is." Again, he was on his knees, with his hands inside the hole in the mattress. I stood in the alcove and watched Fritz at his labor and then the cockatoo strutting around the dying goat. "Aha!" Fritz cried. "More plagues." He yanked and fell back, spilling a cloud of embroidered silk handkerchiefs into the room.

"Hey," I called. "Those are mine. My mother made them."

"How would I know? Have you told me anything?" he grunted. He pulled the handkerchiefs apart and threw them, one by one, into the corner of the room where the dying goat still gasped. The new, uncertain sunlight touched the pile of squares he made so that, when the breeze stirred them, they waved like tiger-butterflies. The goat raised a teeming eyelid, then closed its eye.

"Oh no," Fritz panted, turning to the bed once more. "Not done yet." This time, he fished about a while inside the mattress before he caught something. When he did, he threw his head back, grunted and clenched his teeth. Whatever it was he had caught, it got away from him, but he caught it again. Once more, it got away. The third time he caught it, Fritz held on and, bracing himself against the bed, he pulled. There was a soft, bubbling sound. Something tore and Fritz rolled to one side of the bed, the Persian's ape in his grasp. The animal looked peaceful enough with its arms folded across its chest, its wrinkled face in repose. Fritz got on his knees and looked closely at it. He prodded it with his finger, then, using his thumb and middle finger, he gave such a hard fillip to the tip of its nose that the creature's hands opened spilling a pack of cards. If Fritz expected a miracle, he was disappointed. Nothing happened. The ape was dead.

Getting to his feet, Fritz upended the ape and shook it again and again. When nothing else fell from its body, he flung the creature away. It rolled grotesquely cross the room and came to a stop facing the goat which took that moment to die. "Well, it didn't work," Fritz said as if he were talking to himself. "Sometimes when you shake the damn things, their mechanism starts again."

"It's dead. It's been dead for a long time. I saw it die."

"How would I know, Master of Silence?"

"Please," I said, "hold a couple of those cards to the light and tell me what they say."

"Oh no. I know nothing about any cards. No, Klaus, if silence is the name of your game, I can play it, too."

The pure childishness, as well as the truth, of his reply overwhelmed me. He had been right all along. We were in this tower together. We were both exhausted and lonely. His story had not been an easy one to tell and yet he had risked it. More, he had allowed me to tell parts of it. In what way was the story of my life superior to his simply because I had swathed mine in silence?

Hesitantly, I said, "I'm sorry, Fritz. I've wronged you. Deeply, I'm afraid. Give me a minute and I'll tell . . . "

Fritz yawned, then patted the coverlet of the bed. "Not now, you won't," he said.

What are you going to do?" I asked, alarmed.

He stretched. "What does it look like?" He lay down on the bed.

"You can't go to sleep now. You can't."

"Why not?" His eyes closed with a snap.

"Because . . . because . . . Don't you see. You've won. Because I'm ready to tell you Oh, please, Fritz, don't go to sleep."

He lay there, breathing deeply. From time to time, his uninjured lower lip made erratic, sputtering sounds which in anyone else would have sounded like snores. "Oh, no," I begged. "Fritz, oh Fritz. Wake up. You have to listen. It's time to tell you . . . I want to tell you . . . everything."

XXXIII

FRITZ slept.

"You, Fritz," I called. "I've listened to the story of your life, now you listen to mine."

He slept, but by now, I knew what to do and I did it. I told him everything. Everything. All about my mother's shivering. Her embroidered handkerchiefs. Our meeting with the Persian and saffron vendor. The butcher in the marketplace. The prognosticating cards. The banquet in the castle where my mother died. The death of the ape and the flight of the cockatoo. Hans's rape of the saffron vendor. Our meeting with the Persian in the wood where his beard was clamped in a log.

I told it all in feverish haste, as though, if I could pour it into his ear, the two stories, his and mine, might merge into a whole so illuminating that it would wake him. I talked on and on. My voice grew hoarse; my shoulders drooped. But nothing I said had any effect on Fritz. He slept.

Finally I was exhausted. I kneeled beside him and, putting my head on his chest, I rested.

And it was there that the steady beating of his heart gave me an idea. I decided to search him, but first I had to be sure he was not shamming. I tickled him under the armpits; I blew in his ear; I pricked his toe with the point of my dagger. Nothing happened. He was asleep.

I let my fingers explore his underlinen. I wanted to find the postcard that purported to come from by brother Hans. I had a memory of seeing a young woman reclining under a flowering catalpa tree, but I had been sitting some distance from Fritz so I could not be sure.

My fingers moved over his chest. Sure enough, I found scraps of silk and leather there tied haphazardly to his rags, but the card I wanted eluded me. However, under his left armpit, I did find a small leather pouch tied with a red string. Holding it up to the weak beams of sunlight that now illuminated the tower room I made out three worn gilt letters: R*E*X.

"Well," I said to the sleeping Fritz, "so you haven't quite told me everything." I bit through the string and was startled by the sudden unwinding of a substantial vellum scroll that popped out of the pouch. It was so long, in fact, that I had to allow most of it to trail over the length of Fritz's body and onto the floor at his feet. Across the top of the scroll, written in a bold, masculine hand, was written *A Royal Letter: For Her Eyes Only*.

The handwriting of the letter itself was wretched. Words ran into each other. Lines were ragged. There were spills of ink and smudges over key words, but as far as I could tell, this is what the letter said:

Dear Amy,

Why did it all turn out so badly? I did what I was told to do. I kept my oath to the Witch of the Wood. You *were* offered to be loved. It was an honest offer, more or less. If lust could set you on the mountain, then it could bring you down.

When I woke the image of what I had to do was clear to me. Clear is good, Amy. Add exquisite, limpid, lucid, transparent, crystalline. Then add cool, hard, and smooth and impossible to climb.

Glass!

In my dream, I had seen it first as a rectangle of glass some five miles wide set up vertically in a huge wheat field. The only indication one had that it was there was the inexplicable dark line it created in the middle of the wheat stalks stirring in the breeze and the flashes of light I caught glimpses of as the sun's rays struck the edges of the glass.

As I watched — have I told you, Amy, how sweet the dream was in which I saw all this? — I saw the glass furling, as if some giant hand were making a cornucopia of it. It was a slow and colorful process because as the glass curled, the sunbeams moving through it were refracted, setting off what looked like multi-colored sparks. But that phase passed quickly as what had looked like a cornucopia turned now into a transparent cone, shimmering like a tower carved from a single diamond.

I smiled. What dreamer, seeing what I had just seen, would not sleep the better for it? But then, I understood that I was receiving something more than the gift of a dream. The image of the furling glass in the wheat field was meant to be a sign. In the morning, the meaning of what I had dreamed became clear to me and I went to work at once.

There is a grubby species of beings in the world called engineers and it was to them that I had to have recourse. Oh what a grumbling murmur they set up. "A mile-high mountain of glass!" They pulled at their beards, they pursed their lips, they narrowed their eyes and looked askance at each other. "It is a vast task, your Majesty. A stupendous undertaking, sire. Difficult, difficult, your Highness, perhaps impossible."

In former days, they might have bullied me with their skepticism, but now I would not tolerate it. Was I not the absolute monarch of my realm? Was not the king's word law? And so, rising from my throne I thundered, "Hear and obey. You will build the glass mountain. It will have a circular base with a three-mile circumference; it will have a forty-five-degree slope and it will be a mile high at its tip. It will have a hollow shaft at its center within which a circular stairway to the top will be built. At the apex of the mountain, you will put a throne on which to set the Princess Amalasuntha. Thus, we decree. Build the glass mountain, or your heads will pay the forfeit."

They built it, Amy. Nothing so concentrates the minds of men as a vivid apprehension of their own deaths. So they built it, amazed, in the process, to discover that they were achieving the eighth wonder of the world. My freighters scoured the shores of the island kingdoms in the nearby seas for pure white sand while my miners dug into the bowels of the earth for the soda ash that was required. Meanwhile an army of my peasants reduced the chalk cliffs on the southern coast of my kingdom to rubble to supply by engineers with lime.

Then, there was the building of the structure in which the sand, the soda ash and lime were to be transformed into glass. My engineers constructed it of fire brick and divided it into two sections: the lower one was the furnace while the upper one served as the caldron into which the soda ash, the sand and lime were thrown.

Through a darkened, fire-resistant window I got to watch what transpired during what they called "the melt" inside the caldron.

Amy, there are sights in nature whose grandeur fills the heart with humility: rivers spilling over cliffs to form vast waterfalls; volcanoes erupting, spewing smoke and lava; ocean waves battering a rocky shore; icebergs the size of counties breaking under the sun's caress; islands overwhelmed by tidal waves.

But what I saw through the opaque glass spoke of the grandeur of the human mind. Thought invented the flames that surged through the caldron like waves of the sea. But unlike the ocean's waves, these were unfettered and unrhythmic, flowing in all directions while from above there fell the deluge of sand mixed with soda ash and lime. And where the flame met the sand there was a melding of colors, at first predominantly red, but later shot through with sudden shafts of yellow or streaks of green mottled with white. When the colors had subsided there followed a slow roiling out of which there emerged shapeless organisms that flowed through the flames, gliding in and around and through each other until at last, as if yielding utterly to the heat, they gave up all ambition to achieve form and fused into a gelid mass that flowed slowly toward me at my smoked glass window.

I must confess that at first I was afraid, but all fear left me when I remembered that it was my will that had caused the building of this caldron and ignited its flames. It was I, the king who, having dreamed my dream of glass, had given my skeptical engineers the impetus to make the furnace within whose bowels the glass was being formed. I was the king. I was immune from wrath.

After all, it was my glass, Amy. With it I would satisfy the oath I had sworn to the Witch of the Wood. With it, I would cause to be built a mile-high mountain on whose summit I would put you. Once there, according to my oath, you would be offered to be loved. To another man. Yes, yes. To all other men, if it came to that.

And so, the work went forward, and when it was done, there you were, enthroned at the mountain's top.

And I exulted. The mark on my forehead was gone and I did not have to worry that some heavy-lipped, thick fool was nibbling at your breast. It was a great load off my mind, and I was happy. I felt free and unencumbered. My relief was so great that I commanded revels that lasted for many weeks.

Don't be bitter, Amy. Did you expect me to sit like the chief mourner at a funeral because you were gone?

Ah, no. I felt and looked ten years younger. I drank and laughed and danced. It was an uproarious time, carousing every night. The wine flowed, women cavorted, torches blazed. Even my two most punishing memories—you and Baghdad—receded from my mind. I could recreate my sensual life from a point of innocence, as it were.

For a while, all went well. Then one night, a troupe of gypsies came to the castle. They were a wild, tumultuous crowd. Dark, fierce and musical. Their lead dancer was a pale, black-haired girl who wore a white, low-cut blouse and a scarlet skirt. An amazing creature who whirled to the clatter of tambourines and leaped to the melodies the woodwinds made.

Though she was a little younger than you, she had something of your look. She had firm breasts, sumptuous thighs and a moist sullen smile. Oh it did my heart good to see the wicked light in her eyes.

One night, after I had taken more than my fill of wine, I watched her dancing on a kettle drum. She was doing one of those atrocious dances that comes out of Persia. Her hair was flying, her mouth was open and her hips were gyrating. I could contain myself no longer. Snatching a torch from a servant, I leaped up on the drum and joined her.

We were sensational. Round and round we went, faster and faster. There were cheers; the pace of the music quickened and I found myself whirling in the flickering dreams of my youth. Waving the torch with one hand, I grasped the dancer with the other.

What I had overlooked was that we are all foreigners to the gypsy tribe. My show of lust was deemed an insult to the dancer's virtue. There was an outcry from her father and her brothers and just as I felt myself to be at the very edge of ecstasy, the dancer struck the torch out of my hand. Enraged, I leaped at her.

There was a half-hearted *boom* as the split kettle drum collapsed and we fell. For a moment, we lay still. My head was pressed against the dancer's shoulder; my torch lay guttering on the floor.

At first I thought that nothing much had happened. We had simply tripped and fallen. When I got to my feet and looked around, I was mystified by the look of horror in the faces of my guests. "I'm fine," I started to say. "I'm just fine."

Instead, I shook my head and moaned like a newly wakened idiot. Because the torch, catapulting from my hand, had splashed a drop of oil precisely in the center of my forehead where a small silver mark, no bigger than a coin, was already searing the bone.

Howling, I ran from the tent.

Oh, my servants and my guests followed me, They traced me for a while, but I was not seen again.

Any hunter has seen it happen. He pursues a rabbit which takes a familiar path to its burrow. The hunter follows confidently. The rabbit, made stupid by panic, leaves a track only a fool could lose. Then there is a turn where the rabbit has inexplicably run into a clearing.

And there are no further tracks. None. The trail stops in the clearing. If the hunter finds a bit of fur or a drop of blood, he may guess what happened. Somewhere in the seclusion of the conifers, the great horned owl is digesting.

My tracks, too, ended that way in a clearing. The moonlight through the branches cast a dappled glow. Given the richness of summer and the profusion of delicate pink primroses, blue gentians and yellow rockroses everywhere, the night air should have been filled with summer's sweetest odors.

But oh how the clearing stank. Because there, at its center, there lay what appeared to be a log covered by deadly tiger-butterflies whose wings flickered as they drank and from whose feast there rose a stench like hundreds of dead mice or weeds rotting in marshes.

The men following my trail fell back. Even their dogs grew sick.

They did not find me, Amy. The tiger-butterflies have deadly tongues.

I did love you Amy. Would I have built the glass mountain otherwise?

Signed,

Your father,

R*E*X

XXXIV

IT was a dreadful death. I shuddered and tried not to think of that scene in the moonlight, but I could not rid myself of the image of the tiger-butterflies' black-and-orange wings and their thirsty tongues. In their infancy, they are invisible worms that fly in the night finding out secret joy. Turned into gorgeous adults they are no less ravenous, destroying the dark secret loves on which they feed.

Then a banal and yet important thought occurred to me. Would I be doing the right thing to deliver this letter with its news to Amalasuntha when I found her? True, she had confided her love and her life story to me in the instant when Hans, at the top of the mountain, snatched her up into his saddle just as my white horse sent me crashing to the glass. Still, she might think it was indecorous of me, her lover, to bring her news of the death of a father who was her lover, too.

Meanwhile, there was the rest of the scroll. Having found one interesting account on it, I thought I might as well see what else there was. After only three or four turns of the scroll, I came upon what seemed at first to be a bill of lading. When I looked more closely, I discovered that it was actually a poem written in a tiny and handsome script that reminded me of the penmanship in the journal Fritz's mother kept. The poem, entitled "Two Mothers Rest in Peace," read:

> "Beneath this stone two mothers lie,
> They were not ready, quite, to die.
> Death undid them, one by one,
> Who now lie paired beneath this stone.
>
> Unsteady mothers, here they lie,
> They were no ready, quite to die.
> They lie as close as bone on bone,
> As dark as blindworms under stone.
>
> They loved their sons as mothers do
> Who cannot love the love that's true.
> Beneath this stone, how close they lie
> Who were not ready, quite, to die.
>
> Their thread unwound, they were undone,
> And now lie paired beneath this stone.
> Bound in death, these mothers lie
> Who were not ready, quite, to die."

I laughed and poked Fritz's sleeping form. "Ah, hare-lip," I said, "you move me. More of your work, eh? What a touching tribute. And how cleverly done. Killing two birds, as it were, with one stone with an epitaph that will serve for your mother and mine." Fritz slept on, but, as if to show that he had heard me, there seemed now to be a hint of geniality in his demeanor.

I stretched and yawned. It was a lovely morning and I felt freshly wakened to it, as if a round pleasure, like a cold gooseberry, was poised on my tongue. Through the opening in the tower wall, the sun poured down from a deep

blue sky. Out on the plain, newly sprung bluebells and
yellow gentians opened their cups and smiled back at the
sky in gratitude. Far across the plain, the snow-capped
mountain to the north was bathed in a pale pink light.

Then I looked down at the unwound scroll lying on
Fritz's chest. There was plenty of parchment still left to
unroll. With Fritz's snoring for background, I settled down
to see what I might find. For a while, there was nothing to
read but asterisks. Then legible text appeared and I read:

It's morning. I've been running all night. A few late owls still
float above the trails of unwary mice. The morning sun is struggling to penetrate the mist. Still, there is more than enough light to
see by. For me, two eyes have always been too many for this
world.

Is it clear that I, maimed and exiled, got her? *I* got Amalasuntha. I crested the glass and rode toward her where she stood
with her back to me before the flap of her palanquin adjusting
some article of her clothing. Just as I swept her up before me on
my saddle, my horse took the bit between its teeth and carried us
down the glass. At the bottom, I was disappointed to find no
jubilant crowds, no bands playing, no flying flags.

Fog. Only fog. A thick gray fog through which we rode in
silence. My horse seemed to know just where it was going and
I . . . well, I had Amalasuntha's smell, a mixture of saffron and
lilac, in my nostrils. Tired as I was, I dozed in the saddle and
dreamed of her beauty.

It was some time later that we entered the tundra and I knew
we were in the country of the Lapps. Amalasuntha shifted in my
arms and I woke with a start. I looked around and saw nothing but
emptiness. "My God," I thought, "what shall we do here?" Then I
felt the pressure of Amalasuntha's thighs against my knees.

My heart beat furiously. In a moment, I would gaze into her
lovely face. My flesh would glow. Meanwhile, what I said was,

"Princess, may I help you down? After this long ride, you must be tired."

"Thank you." Her voice was low and gentle. "You are kind."

Letting my reins drop, I dismounted and helped her down. She was strangely heavy, but I managed to set her on the turf. When I reached for my bridle, my horse moved out of reach. "Pardon me, princess," I said, and went to catch the creature. The sly beast waited for me until my fingers had all but closed over its reins, then it walked away again.

I chased my horse for the longest time, but always it escaped me. I could almost swear that it regarded me with pity, even as it enticed and eluded me. I don't know how much longer this futile game would have continued if my horse had not heard the sound of whinnying mares or stallions on the slope of the distant mountain. Pricking up its ears it loped off to answer that implacable call.

Worn, bedraggled, my mouth filled with dust, my feet bruised and my boots badly scuffed, I made my way back to Amalasuntha.

In the mist, she was an indistinct figure on the hillock of peat before which she stood. "Forgive me, princess," I said. "I'm sorry to tell you that we are now without a mount."

"Yes?" She waited and I, out of respect, waited too. Minutes passed. The cold morning air made me shiver, then I felt the touch of her finger on my thumb. "Prince," she said. "I've been on the mountain for a long, long time. We are wasting daylight."

I did not need to be urged. I sprang forward and, despite a sudden sharp smell in my nostrils of furze mingled with some personal odor of her own, I had her in my arms.

She was Amalasuntha for whose sake so many thousands of young men had died! Amalasuntha, woman without flaw, woman unattainable. And I had attained her. Whether it was because, as an innocent, I had been blessed, or whether, by my superiority I had been able to bend the universe to my will, the fact is, she was in my arms. She was mine.

It was a moment so sublime that I could hardly move, indeed, did not want to move lest I should spoil it by some crude earth-bound gesture.

Neither of us, however, could avoid breathing, and so it was that I became conscious of a delicate wheezing from her lungs. Then I smelled again that whiff of furze. This time, the more personal odor that had accompanied it was stronger.

Is it clear that when I snatched her up on the glass mountain her back had been turned to me? Is it clear, too, that, though we had traveled for hours together, and though she was now in my arms, I had not actually seen her?

Slowly, carefully, I drew back. Only a little, but enough so that she noticed it and stiffened. I closed my eyes. My hand moved through her coarse hair, then over her wrinkled forehead. My irresolute finger stroked leather skin, discovered craggy cheekbones, bristles, moles, and wens. Amalasuntha!

"Are you afraid?" she whispered. "Don't be. I can make you happy." My hand traveled over the warts, the knobs, the pits, the hairy outline of her upper lip. She sighed. "Be careful with me. You won't hurt me, I know."

"Let me go," I whispered.

"Stay with me," she said.

"Oh, no."

The grip of her fingers on my wrist entered the bone. "Don't leave me," she urged. "I *am* Amalasuntha." Then, wretchedly, "I am, you know."

In a hollow voice, I replied, "It doesn't matter."

"It does," she whispered. Weak beams of sunlight penetrated the mist. "Oh prince, if you could be patient you would learn to know me beyond the touch of your fingers."

"How can I deny what my fingers . . . know?" I held my breath.

Her laugh cut through the mist. "What do they know? They don't know *me*. Oh, how I wish you could see me as I am. As I have seen myself bending over pools under flowering almond trees. My hair, you know, is black and long."

Through my shoes, I could feel the springy furze. As an ugly man, or as an exile, I should have known how she felt, but, unable to deny what my fingertips had taught me, I backed away.

"Stay," she said. "You could make me beautiful." Her voice sounded fragile, as if, in it, pride were threatened by humiliation. For one moment, I had an impulse to run to her; to enfold her again in my arms, and to cover her face with kisses. Her face!

I began to run, but her voice reached me. "I *am* Amalasuntha, you know. As clean and natural as a pebble. Only a little more courage and you will have your heart's desire. Just one kiss. A single kiss. Not even freely given. A kiss under compulsion. Holding you breath, if you like . . ."

I ran. I prayed and ran. Over the tundra there hung an immense stillness into which I flung my prayers. The faster I ran, the more fervently I prayed. Often I stumbled and scuffed my shoes.

The word "kiss" was the last word to reach me. Hearing it, I spat and wiped my sleeve against my mouth and ran.

I left her there in the mist which the weak light of the sun was just beginning to penetrate. I left her there, alone.

XXXV

I ROLLED up the scroll and tied it again with its scarlet thread.

Fritz slept on his wretched bed. There was such a torrent of sunlight in the room now that I was afraid it would wake him but, though it shone full on his eyelids, he slept on, one arm dangling over the edge of the bed, the other crooked over his chest. His fist was jammed against his ragged mouth.

On the floor, the cockatoo had commenced to strut indecently, pecking at my mother's handkerchiefs, at the dead billy goat, at the ape's tiny balled fists. Sometimes the bird paused beside the bed to scold the sleeper; I loathed its neatness, its whiteness, its martinet's swagger and arrogance. I got to my feet with the idea that it would take but a moment to wring its neck. Out of the corner of my eye, I saw the complicated doorway through which I had made my way into the room last night. There was nothing to keep me from running down the long staircase to the flower-studded plain below. My eyes glistened at the idea. The spittle in my mouth tasted sweet and fresh. But first, I had to kill the bird.

Fritz snorted. The cockatoo, offended by the sound, fluttered away from the bed and perilously close to me. Cautiously, I bent toward it, but a stray beam of sunlight striking one of its eyes startled the bird and it took off on a wild sweep around the room, bruising itself on the bed, on the wall, on the stone doorway. Finally, it came to rest, perched on one of the billy goat's horns. I went after it. The bird made a cautionary chirp as if to warn me away, but I leaped at it with the force of all my weight. I missed and fell, crashing across the goat. When I sat up, I had a handful of maggoty hair in my clutch.

I flung the stuff away and got to my feet. The bird was in my mother's handkerchiefs. "Don't you dare," I growled and dived at it. But a man as fat as I am dives at his peril. I missed again and fell beside the bed. "Slowly," I cautioned. "Do it slowly. Patience rides a faster horse than haste." Very slowly, I got to my feet. There was the cockatoo, perched now on Fritz's chest. I took a deep breath and inched forward. The bird watched me pertly. "Leave him alone," I said. "Let the poor man sleep."

The bird clucked as I leaped but the exertion proved too much for me. The blood drained from my head and I lost consciousness. When I opened my eyes, I saw that I was lying on Fritz. The cockatoo was in my fist, its destroyed heart still pulsing under my fingertips. I sat up and examined its blood-smeared body. On one of its thin legs a slender vial was tied with a blue thread. Cutting the thread, I removed the vial, then I flung the bird out of the opening in the tower.

I held the vial up to the light and could just make out that there was paper of some sort rolled up in it. I pounded the vial into my palm but I could not make the paper fall out. Putting the vial between my teeth, I bit down. The crushed glass made my upper lip bleed. I spat the bits of glass out, then, swallowing the blood that welled into my mouth, I made myself comfortable against Fritz's chest and unwound what turned out to be a letter. It said:

Dear Prince,

Where are you?

I am at the top of a glass mountain in the ten-mile square just north of where you are. Here, the stars feel as baffled as I do but they continue to wheel in their courses. They are obtuse and bright and patient. They endure.

A little courage in the face of squeamishness and you would have had your heart's desire. Amalasuntha. The most beautiful woman in the world. One kiss. Not even freely given.

Never mind. There will always be an undaunted youth who finds his way to the top of the luminous mountain. One day, he will crest the glass and catch me up on the crupper of his saddle. Then, when he has carried me to some quiet corner of the universe, he will rein in his horse. He will set me down on a clump of furze and then. Ah, then there will be kisses. Kisses. Perhaps, even yours.

Amalasuntha

As I refolded the letter, I wondered where she had found the crystal vial in which she had enclosed it and how it had come to be tied to the cockatoo's thin leg.

Fritz, against whom I am leaning, stirs. Thinking that he may be waking, I call, "Hey, Fritz." Nothing happens. He sleeps.

I unbutton his shirt and loosen his belt so that he may be more comfortable in the advancing heat of the day. Outside, somewhere in the flower-studded plain below, a rooster, badly misinformed about the time of day, crows: "Cock-a-doodle-dooooooo."

Fritz sleeps. He snores with both his nose and mouth. He breathes in through his mouth with such gusto that his lips tremble then he breathes out through his nose with a sound like a saw cutting through green wood.

Tenderly, I take his boots off and put them beside the bed. Carefully, I help him to lie on one side of the torn reed coverlet so that I can lie beside him on the other. Fat though I am, there is room. Now he lies dry and warm. I hold him easily, with his head on my shoulder.

There is something still left to do. I am fat Klaus and he is harelipped Fritz. We have shared a night and a morning. Touching his ruined upper lip with my finger, I say, "Are you ready, Fritz?"

He says nothing, but both his ruined and his lower lip tremble. The sight is not a pleasant one but I do not turn away. Instead, I sit up and take his head between my hands. His breathing quickens as if he would warn me. He has a point. A kiss is no casual matter. Moistening my lips, I ready myself, then I bend and kiss him full on his fragmented mouth.

A groan fills the room. Whether it is his or mine, I do not know. I kiss harder, even as I feel his shoulder squirming against my arm. I know I may not close my eyes. I kiss. He turns and fights and I hold a broad-faced, placid woman in whose eyes forgiveness wells. "Stay with me," she says. "We can be happy here. I am a witch, not a whore." I dry her tears with my hand, but I keep my lips on hers. I hold her tight. I kiss.

A low wind touches the corners of the room. Outside, there is the sound of birds and now I hold the Persian in my arms. I can feel the touch of his beard against my cheek and smell his cleanly smell. "Good," he whispers. "Hold on. You have a lovely kiss. See, It only takes a little patience. Kiss, boy. Kiss." I taste his words. I kiss, but now it is a small fat woman to whose lips I cling. From her mouth there comes the tainted breath of birds. For Fritz' sake, for mine, I kiss and hold her close. Her mouth under my lips says, "Birds are easier to love. They can be counted on to fly." I hold her tight and kiss until an irritable king moans in my embrace, "Where did you learn those embraces, Amy? Who taught you how to move?" I will not let him go though he is wiry and furious. I kiss, my mouth against his neatly trimmed mustache. He twists and lashes out at me and I find my mother in my arms. Her kiss is languid, icy. She is my mother and I kiss as if my mouth could tell her something. I want to say, "There's no need to shiver, mother," but I dare not spoil my kissing with a word. I kiss, and when she slips away and the saffron-vendor is in my arms, I hardly need to shift the pressure of my lips. There is a scent of lilacs, roses, dogwood or acacia. I kiss and hold her close and wonder if I dare ask her pardon for what my brother did and what I dreamed, but now there's only kissing to be done and when she slips away, there's my brother Hans in my arms. Distaste shows in his face. He would prefer lips other than mine, but we may not escape each other. He smells of honeysuckle and of sage. I hold him close, I kiss and the look on his face changes from contempt to soft bewilderment. I cling and kiss. Then I have the miller's daughter in my embrace. She twists and jerks and begs for Baldur whose lips are next pressed to mine. Mistaking me for my mother, he begs so pitifully, "Take back your heart," that I would freely give him mine, but now, I have no hope but kissing. He groans and turns away and in my arms another body rolls. I tighten my grasp to resist the iron strength coiling and pulling at me. I hold fast, searching the indistinct face against which my lips are pressed for features that I might know. I kiss and pray. We roll, incapable of melting into each other or of staying apart; and he is now above me, pressing down on me with his enormous weight. It is almost more than I can endure, but I kiss because the weight against my chest is me. There is a fragrance in the room of crocus flowers. I kiss and find Amalasuntha at my lips. I have her now. Wild and shapely and fragrant as heather. I kiss. My lips are bleeding. An ant is walking across her cheek. I long to kill it with my tongue, but there's no time for anything but kisses and arriving at our journeys end. There's a burst of fragrant amaranth, the flower that blooms forever. We kiss, we fall together, Fritz and Klaus. We emerge into a dazzling world in which we have not lost each other. My eyes are on his face. His lips have never left my torn sweet mouth.